STORIES ABOUT Mothers and Their Daughters & The Clock Family

BETH CAROL SOLOMON

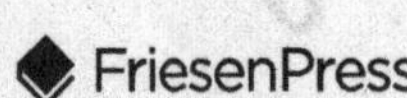

One Printers Way
Altona, MB R0G 0B0
Canada

www.friesenpress.com

First Edition — 2021

ISBN
978-1-03912-133-1 (Hardcover)
978-1-03912-132-4 (Paperback)
978-1-03-912134-8 (eBook)

1. Fiction, Short Stories (Single Author)

Distributed to the trade by The Ingram Book Company

TABLE OF CONTENTS

In honor of my Mom

and in memory of my Dad who taught me

what love and family are all about

PART ONE

Mothers and Their Daughters

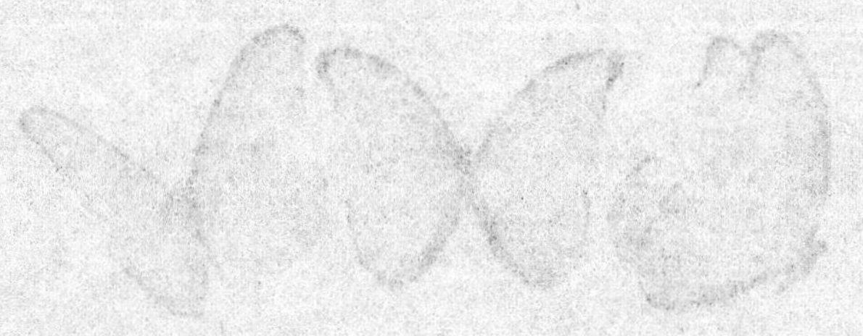

MY ELLEN, MY DARLING DAUGHTER

Peggy Ella, smiling, turned from the sink as she was drying a plate, watching her daughter, Ellen, playing happily with her dolls. Ellen, not quite two years old and blind from birth, was generally a very happy and gleeful little girl. She was not fussy or demanding, nor did she cry much. She loved to be picked up and cuddled. When she was, she would giggle with delight. It did not seem to bother her that she was unable to see.

Peggy Ella, with long blonde curly hair and hazel eyes, loved being her mother. Ellen was such an easy baby to love. A joy! Ellen had short blonde hair, her curls cut close to her head, clad in a white sundress with small red daisies, and wearing open-toe white sandals. Peggy Ella just loved observing every little move her daughter made. She could not get enough of her, and soaked in every single aspect of her, morning, noon, and night.

Then Peggy Ella turned back to the sink resuming to drying the rest of the dishes. Still smiling, happily singing to herself.

Suddenly, Peggy Ella heard a piercing scream, and jumped, nearly dropping the plate she was drying. She was frightened. Her heart, heavy, nearly jumped out of her skin, quivering and shaking. A tight, sharp pain ran down her spine. She had a knot in her stomach. "What happened?!" Peggy Ella shrieked.

Ellen was screaming, tears in her sightless eyes, at the top of her lungs.

"What's the matter, Ellen, my darling?" Peggy Ella could not understand. This was not typical behavior for Ellen. She was scared out of her wits.

"Ma-a-a-ma!" she blurted out, struggling hysterically.

"Ma-a-a-ma!" she shrieked again, struggling for air. She did not stop screaming piercingly, unable to stop and catch her breath.

Ellen held up one of her dolls with one hand, while holding the doll's arm with the other.

"What's wrong?" Peggy Ella asked, concerned, while gently holding her shoulders, trying to soothe her.

Peggy Ella saw the doll and its arm. She surmised what the problem was. "The arm broke off the doll?" she asked, earnestly and quietly.

Ellen stopped crying, gulping for breath, trying to get composed and calm. Tearfully, she managed, while nodding, "Y-y-y-es!"

"Let Mama fix it, okay?" Ellen touched her mother's mouth, feeling her smile.

Peggy Ella took the doll and its arm over to the counter, opened a drawer, took out a roll of tape, and wrapped the doll's arm back on, making sure it was secure and tight.

"There!" Peggy Ella stated proudly. "All done. Just like new!"

She brought the doll back to her daughter. Ellen felt the spot where the arm broke and knew it was taken care of. Everything was wonderful. Mama, the fixer of everything. Problem solved. Ellen smiled and laughed. Peggy Ella did also. She had come to her daughter's rescue. Mama, her heroine!

Both mother and daughter embraced and kissed each other. All smiles and giggles.

"My Ellen, my darling daughter! I love you all the way to Pluto and back!"

"Me, too!" Ellen rejoiced with love and understanding, smiling, while feeling her mother's gleeful facial expression.

A wonderful day forever.

A MOTHER'S UNCONDITIONAL LOVE FOR HER MENTALLY CHALLENGED DAUGHTER

Darlena Jo was indignant while speaking on the telephone to Miss Lorme, her daughter's resource teacher. Tammy Jo had been going for extra help with her schoolwork. Miss Lorme had told Darlena Jo that Tammy Jo needed to be placed in a special class for the educable mentally challenged. She refused to believe it.

"She's just a little slow. I'll spend time with her work."

Tammy Jo was thirteen years old, with shoulder-length, wavy, mousy brown hair. Her eyes were watery, her nose perky, her lips like rosebuds.

"My daughter is not—is not impaired!" she insisted adamantly. "She'll be in a regular class. I'll help her."

Miss Lorme resignedly, responded: "All right."

Thus, Tammy Jo went to the junior high school. And each day, Darlena Jo saw by her daughter's sad face that nothing was going right. She was having problems. When her mother would ask her calmly, quietly, and gently, Tammy Jo would not respond. Her face was always teary-eyed and gloomy. But Darlena Jo would continue to help her with her schoolwork. However, after all their hard work, Tammy Jo never brought any papers home. She threw them away.

Finally, after one week, Tammy Jo came home crying bitterly, tears streaming down her face. She gulped uncontrollably while hiccupping.

Darlena Jo, gently, put her hands on the sides of her face and asked softly, "What's the matter?"

She looked into her eyes earnestly.

Tammy Jo, bursting into loud weeping, managed to say, "Everybody bothers me! The boys threw my books and pocketbook on the floor. Another boy threw balls of paper at me and kept shooting spitballs at me. Another boy kept pulling on my pocketbook. Another boy grabbed my hat off my head and threw it on the floor. Another boy kicked me between the legs and hit me, another kept kicking my desk with his foot, another kept kicking the back of my chair while I was struggling with a difficult exam. And all the girls laughed hysterically, calling me a crazy psycho and a mental moron. And the teacher puts me on the section sheet every single day. She lets everybody bother me and says that no one is bothering me when I would tell her what the other children do. She yells at me and calls me a young lady!" She kept gulping relentlessly, trying to compose and control herself. Darlena Jo put her arms around her shoulders, hugging her closely to her breast.

"I'll go up to school tomorrow. I will take care of it. No one will ever hurt you again. I promise."

The next day came. Mother and daughter went up to school. Tammy Jo went to class and Darlena Jo indignantly went up to Tammy Jo's teacher, confronting her. Nonchalantly and tiredly, the teacher said, "Children can be very cruel at this age—especially to a child as challenged as your daughter. She needs to be in Mr. Bruce's class with children who will not make fun of her."

Glaring at the teacher, Darlena Jo turned and went back home.

The minute she entered her home, she heard the telephone. She picked up the receiver. It was the principal informing her that Tammy Jo was not seen in school. The teachers told him that she was not in any of her classes.

Darlena Jo figured it out. Her daughter must have snuck out of the school somehow. Thus, she called the police frantically. With panic in her voice, she hysterically blurted out that Tammy Jo had disappeared from school.

After hanging up the telephone, it dawned on her that, indeed, Tammy Jo needed special help. She was different, her mother admitted to herself. She did love her deeply. She had thought that admitting this would show and mean she did not accept her daughter's special needs and that she could not love her because of her disability. But she did. She did love her.

Unconditionally. It did not matter that she was mentally challenged. Tammy Jo was a warm, quiet, caring, loving daughter.

Suddenly, the doorbell rang. Darlena Jo opened it and saw two policemen.

"We found her, Mrs. Prescott. She was hiding in some bushes. A neighbor called, saying she heard loud crying, and there she was," one policeman pointed out.

Standing behind him, Tammy Jo appeared with her tear-stained face, and cried out bitterly, "Mama! Mama!"

Darlena Jo went up to her and held her hands.

"Everything is all right, my darling daughter. Mama's not angry."

Tammy Jo still sobbed, but was composed. "Please don't make me go back to that place anymore!"

"I won't. You will be in a class with other children like yourself. They will not make fun of you. I promise."

A slight smile crossed her daughter's face.

"Really, Mama?"

"Yes, my darling daughter." She hugged Tammy Jo to her bosom for comfort.

"Now, would you like some milk and cookies? They are on the table. Also, would you like a kitten? Miss Lorme's cat gave birth to five kittens the other day. We'll go tomorrow after school, okay?" Darlena Jo smiled, looking lovingly into her daughter's eyes.

Tammy Jo's face burst out into a wide smile, her eyes shining like stars. It was the first time in a long while that she had something to be happy about.

"Yes, Mama, yes!" she exclaimed.

Together, swinging hand in hand, then clasping their arms around their waists, they walked into the kitchen.

THE NEXT DAY

Darlena Jo and Tammy Jo walked down the corridor and turned their heads toward Tammy Jo's new class.

"This is it," Darlena Jo showing the classroom door to her daughter.

They entered the classroom, seeing Mr. Bruce teaching a math lesson. His students watched with earnest interest.

Suddenly, he turned around and saw Darlena Jo and Tammy Jo. He greeted them with a gleaming smile, "How are we doing, ladies?"

With her hands on her daughter's shoulders, Darlena Jo introduced her. "This is my daughter, Tammy Jo, who you were expecting today."

Mr. Bruce extended his hand to Tammy Jo, and she took it. "Welcome to my class."

Then, he turned toward his students and announced, "Class, this is your new classmate, Tammy Jo. Please make her feel welcome."

Together, in unison, the students greeted her eagerly: "Hello, Tammy Jo."

Mr. Bruce led her to a seat next to a freckle-faced girl with wavy, red hair, Starletta, who smiled pleasantly at her, and vice versa.

Mr. Bruce instructed the class to continue with their math lesson while he spoke to Darlena Jo.

"She'll be all right, Mrs. Prescott," he assured her, firmly but gently. "Nice meeting you. Have a good day."

Darlena Jo smiled and waved at her daughter, blowing her a kiss. "I love you, my darling daughter, all the way to Pluto and back."

Tammy Jo joyfully responded, waving her hand, "Me, too, Mama. See you later."

Darlena Jo exited the class. Mr. Bruce resumed the math lesson.

Tammy Jo saw her work and textbooks on her desk. She glanced through them puzzledly. Two other girls turned and offered to help her. One girl, Paulette, with short, straight, ash-blonde hair, a pink headband, and hazel eyes, and the other, Dinah, with straight, shoulder-length dirty blonde hair and blue-green eyes, volunteered to help her get settled. Tammy Jo graciously thanked them.

At the end of the class, Starletta, Paulette, and Dinah invited Tammy Jo to walk home with them. She was ecstatic, for she never had friends before.

She told them about her kitten, Artemis, an orange tabby, that her mother promised her this evening. Her new friends told her funny stories on their way home. They agreed to go to each other's houses. It was a lot to take in, but Tammy Jo did not mind. She had real friends now.

When she arrived at her house, she turned and waved goodbye to the girls gleefully. Afterward, she bounced in through the door excitedly, throwing her backpack on the floor, running wildly into her mother's arms.

"Mama, Mama! I have three real, real friends." She was talking so fast she was nearly out of breath.

Her mother gently took her hands into hers, patting them affectionately. "Slow down, honey," she cautiously advised her daughter.

Tammy Jo told her about her day in her new class and her three girlfriends. Her first ones.

"Oh, Tammy Jo!" Her mother exclaimed delightedly. "I am so happy for you." Her large, brown eyes sparkled brightly. She loved her daughter so. And vice versa.

Together, they headed toward the kitchen table. Three chocolate chip cookies and a full glass of milk were on the table.

When Tammy Jo began eating her snacks, Darlena Jo watched her proudly, with much love. Tammy Jo then looked up and smiled back.

It was an exceptionally good day. Today and always.

For they loved each other unconditionally. Forever.

It did not bother Darlena Jo that her daughter would always be mentally challenged. She would never be a doctor, a lawyer, a CEO, or a president of a conglomerate. She was not a genius and would always encounter a lot more obstacles and struggles than her peers; though her upbeat, gleeful spirit never gave in to defeat. She would be facing challenges in her life. No one could say what the future held for her daughter. Only time would tell, and whatever she did later in life was in God's hands.

But she was happy. She was a kind, loving, quiet, gentle child who took responsibility for her cat. She fed it, cleaned out its litter box, and gave it bowls of fresh, cold water. She constantly picked it up, caressed and held it, petting it close to her bosom, whispering kind, tender words.

Also, every day, Tammy Jo would tell her mother: "You're so pretty, Mama." It did not matter how her mother looked or felt. She did go to the beauty parlor every week to get her short, thick, blonde hair done in waves surrounding her face. Not a hair out of place. Even when she was under the weather and things seemed dismal and hopeless, Tammy Jo's spirited nature lifted her up and made her feel she was dancing on air and glad to be alive.

"Don't worry, Mama. Everything is already good. Keep smiling."

And she did.

Thus, Darlena Jo considered herself to be lucky and blessed to have such a wonderful daughter as Tammy Jo.

However, there was one aspect of their lives that never seemed to arise. James Ferdinand—Darlena Jo's husband and Tammy Jo's father.

James had planned to become a criminal justice lawyer as his life's profession. He had graduated from Harvard at the top of his class. Unfortunately, during his first year as an associate, he had died from a heart attack. They had barely been married two years and Tammy Jo had not been even a year old. His death had been sudden, for he had always been healthy, and there had been no history of heart problems in his family that he had known about. He had loved his wife and baby daughter immensely and left them with a large insurance policy to help them.

Even with that, Darlena Jo wanted to do something—not for financial reasons, but because she enjoyed keeping busy. So, she decided to go to art school to learn how to paint. She was highly creative. Besides, she was told she had an artistic bend. Also, she wanted to teach art part-time and inspire others as she had been inspired.

That early evening, after dinner, Tammy Jo, clad in a long, pink floral, cotton nightdress called to her mother, who was wearing the same nightdress—mother-daughter nightdresses. She had a picture in her hands.

"Mama?" she called.

Darlena Jo turned around after wiping down the counters and smiled lovingly.

Tammy Jo held up a photograph of James – her father. He had thick, wavy black hair, deep, twinkling blue eyes, and a bright smile with pearly-white teeth.

"Tell me about Daddy," she requested of her mother with intense inquisitiveness.

"Certainly," her mother obliged.

Mother and daughter laid back on the living room couch. Tammy Jo rested in her mother's arms while she stroked her hair tenderly.

The talk began. With love. As always.

Darlena Jo began.

"Daddy loved you so very much. You were the heart of his heart, his light. You were such a beautiful baby—a quiet, docile bundle with such bright, sharp blue eyes, always gazing around with curiosity. He'd be so proud of you." She gazed and sighed awesomely at her daughter, who looked up at her with a bright sparkle in her eyes.

She continued.

LAURIE JO, DAUGHTER OF MY HEART

The class was working quietly on an assignment. Laurie Jo, clad in a long sleeved white T-shirt with brown denim overalls, a brown leather jacket hung on the back of her chair, was struggling. For she was writing furiously and fiercely, holding her pencil on her paper. She was shaking, her body making jerky, twisty motions. Her classmates did their work calmly. Polly Harrington, their fifth-grade teacher, while sitting at her desk, glanced up and saw Laurie Jo, uptight and tense, her face in a contorted rage, cheeks burning red. Mrs. Harrington got up and walked toward her desk, gently patting her hand on her wrist.

"Are you all right, dear?" she asked softly.

No response or sign of acknowledgement came from her.

"Class," she addressed firmly, her body erect and slender, standing tall, her deep, dark brown hair in a French twist, her large, brown eyes bright, her nose long and thin, her pinkish lips not too thin or thick—just perfect, her hands soft and smooth. One could take a photograph, for her features were perfect. She was as physically attractive as her personality was loving and kind; she had the patience of a saint, was firm but gentle, and understanding of all her students, regardless of their individual challenges. Everyone loved her.

"I have to go to a meeting now. I'm expecting all of you to be on your honor and to behave yourselves." She turned to two other girls and stated, "Anita, Suzanne, you two will be in charge. If there is a problem, please bring it to my attention. But I hope and trust there will not. I'm hoping you will all comply."

Then she faced the girls. "I have confidence in you girls. You are my best two students, and I know I could depend on you, all right, girls?"

They nodded in agreement, with a smile. "Yes, Mrs. Harrington, we won't let you down."

Anita had straight, light brown hair that ended slightly above her shoulders; pearly hazel eyes; a bright smile always on her perky lips; and a little, pudgy and stout nose.

Suzanne had long, straight, dark brown hair that hung on her shoulders, a flat nose, and wide lips. Also, she had a sparkling smile.

Mrs. Harrington smiled at them, then reached for her handbag and left the room. Some of the students looked up making sure their teacher was out of earshot, smirked and turned toward the others.

"Okay, everybody!" One boy got up and motioned to the class, calling out loud, "Let's go!"

All the students jumped out of their seats, rushing up to Laurie Jo, and pushed all her books on the floor, laughing hysterically as hyenas. Another kicked the side of her desk with her foot. Laurie Jo screamed murderously, bursting into tears.

"Leave me alone!" she cried out, again and again.

Another student grabbed her book bag and threw all its contents across the room. Some boys shot spitballs. One boy was kicking and banging the back of her chair with his feet. Some girls jeered and sneered arrogantly: "Psycho, psycho, psychopath!" They danced around her and pushed her against the back wall.

She hit her head as she fell backward. "Crazy fuckin' bitch!" They continued relentlessly, without mercy. Laurie Jo's face turned beet red from her uncontrollable, endless shrieking. The whole class was in an uproar.

Anita and Suzanne were appalled and indignant. Anita walked over to one of the boys and ordered, "Leave her alone, you prick!" She pushed him backward with her hands. He almost fell. Then she held up her fist to him and threatened, "You see this, asshole?"

Suzanne went over to the girls with indignance and staunchly said, "Hey, you stupid ingrates." She glared at them, "You leave her alone this instant or you'll have me to deal with!" She proudly and triumphantly grinned.

The girls haughtily laughed and asked, "What are you going to do about it? Are you going to make me? You love her or something?"

Anita screamed back, "What if we do, you fuckin' cunt?!" She kicked the girl between her legs and pushed her down on the floor. The girl screamed. "OW!"

"Good," Suzanne announced victoriously.

Then Anita went over to the boys, pushing and kicking them forcibly. They fell into a heap on the floor.

Both girls stood there, with their arms across their chests, gleaming with joy. They watched their classmates yelling and screaming, holding themselves while groaning with pain. Anita and Suzanne had won—they got what they wanted: justice for their friend, Laurie Jo.

Anita and Suzanne added, "You all deserve to rot in hell, because you're all a bunch of mother fuckin' bastards! God will get you—get you all!"

"Anita," Suzanne faced her friend, "Please, go get Mrs. Harrington in here immediately!" Anita dashed out the room. The teasing ceased, but the students snickered mockingly, looking around the room, glancing at each other, still laughing amongst themselves.

"Class!!!" Mrs. Harrington shouted angrily while banging the hall pass on her desk. Her large brown eyes blazed furiously, like they were on fire.

Quickly, the students turned, facing their teacher. No one made a sound.

"I'm ashamed of every one of you. Making fun of a classmate—especially one that is weak and defenseless, who never did a thing to you. You are all very cruel and heartless, and I am ashamed to have you all in my class." She turned toward each student, eyes boiling with rage.

"You, Nathan!" The boy looked up. "Wipe that stupid smirk off your face! Now!!" she snapped.

Then she turned to another student—a girl with long, straight, blonde hair and blue eyes, who was giggling and smiling to herself. "Young lady! You find this amusing? You think it's funny—a big joke?!" The girl looked down solemnly, painfully cowering her head down on her desk.

The class became silent and scared. Not one word was said, and no one made a move. They sat at their desks like statues. Mrs. Harrington stood there, speechless. She removed her eyeglasses, which hung from her chain, and faced Anita and Suzanne.

"You two did an incredibly good job today. I am deeply sorry you had to deal with this situation, but you handled it well. Laurie Jo is extremely fortunate to have friends like you two. Laurie Jo needed support and you were exceedingly kind to show her compassion."

Then, facing the class, Mrs. Harrington staunchly stated, "Anita and Suzanne have all your your names. Punishment will be detention for two weeks after school. None of you will be participating in any extracurricular activities during that time. Your parents will be notified. And, lastly, all of you will write, 'I will never tease Laurie Jo again and I am sorry I was mean, cruel, and heartless,' one hundred times. 'And I am ashamed of myself.' Your parents will sign it, and it will have to be on my desk first thing tomorrow morning."

The students sat at their desks mournfully, not uttering a syllable or moving a bone in their bodies.

Mrs. Harrington announced flatly, "Class is dismissed." They gathered their books and backpacks while exiting the class.

"Laurie Jo," Mrs. Harrington motioned gently to her, "please come up to me and sit down."

She quietly complied.

Mrs. Harrington put her hand on her cheek and softly said, "Don't be frightened. You did nothing wrong."

Laurie Jo just sat, saying nothing, as she stared mournfully in her teacher's eyes.

"I will call your mother," she began. At this, Laurie Jo got scared, and screeched, holding her hands to her stomach.

"Don't be afraid," her teacher reassured her. "I will tell her you are having having difficulties with your classwork. You are a very bright, well-behaved, and sweet girl, and you do try extremely hard. However, I have noticed that you seem to have trouble with reading and writing. Your oral work is outstanding, and you participate well in group discussions. I will make an appointment with her to discuss it after school tomorrow. We're going to help you."

Laurie Jo fidgeted nervously in her seat, with her head down. Again, Mrs. Harrington put her hand under her chin.

"No one is angry with you. You're a good and lovely girl, and I'm proud to have you in my class."

At that, Laurie Jo slowly looked up, with a weak smile on her face.

"We'll see that she gets home safely, Mrs. Harrington," the girls proclaimed.

Mrs. Harrington pleasantly winked at the girls.

Suzanne and Anita stood on each side of Laurie Jo while walking out the door.

"She'll be fine," they assured their teacher, who agreeably smiled.

"I know. I have faith in both of you."

"Come with us," Anita led Laurie Jo out.

. "We'll always be with you," Suzanne added.

The three girls left together, their arms around each other. Mrs. Harrington was contented as she watched them from the window heading to the school bus. She was happy Laurie Jo had made friends—probably the first she had ever had.

While they were on the bus, sitting together, Suzanne turned toward Laurie Jo and gracefully said, "Don't let anyone intimidate you. You are much better than they are. Always smile and laugh. There's nothing wrong with you."

Then Anita chimed in, "We'll always be by your side. You're not alone anymore."

Laurie Jo smiled a short smile, but with glee. She nodded to her new friends and mentioned, "I'll be getting off soon. My house is on the next corner."

"Anita and I live about two blocks away, but we will get off with you just to make sure you're safe. Is your mother home, Laurie Jo? We just want her to know you're fine, all right?" Suzanne reiterated sincerely.

Laurie Jo nodded. The bus came to a halt. The three girls got off and walked with Laurie Jo toward her home to meet her mother.

Anita rang the bell. They waited until there was an answer. Laurie Jo's mother opened the door and glanced at her daughter and puzzledly at the girls, concerned, seeing her daughter's tear-stained face and red eyes. She took her daughter's face in her hands and plaintively asked,

"What happened? What is the matter? What's wrong, my darling daughter of my heart?"

Laurie Jo didn't respond, but threw her arms around her mother's neck, crying bitterly, "Mama! Mama!"

Anita volunteered, "Mrs. Wentworth, everybody in our class was tormenting her when Mrs. Harrington left the room. They teased her mercilessly by kicking her, throwing her books and backpack on the floor, shooting spitballs at her, pushing her desk over, and kicking the back of her chair. Also, they called her cruel names." She had to stop to catch her breath.

"It was awful, Mrs. Wentworth," Suzanne went on. "They wouldn't stop. Honest, Mrs. Wentworth," she said pleadingly.

Anita resumed, "I had to get Mrs. Harrington to come back to class at once."

"She did," Suzanne affirmed.

"The whole class got punished. And we reassured her that we'll help Laurie Jo and make sure she is fine."

Marion Jo smiled at the girls, thanking them profusely, grateful her daughter had such nice girls as friends.

"Would you like to come in and have a glass of milk and brownies, girls?" she offered.

The two girls smiled, but politely declined her invitation.

"Thanks, that is very kind of you, Mrs. Wentworth, but we have to go home now."

They called out to Laurie Jo while waving, "Goodbye, Laurie Jo! See you in class tomorrow!"

With a sweet, small smile, she managed to say, "Okay, thank you. Bye, now."

Marion Jo closed the door and tended to her daughter. Gently, she put her hand on her wrist, saying with love, "I love you and everything will be fine. I will not let anyone, or anything hurt you. You have my word. You are a good girl and I love you very, very much. You know that, my darling daughter of my heart?"

Laurie Jo nodded at her mother, "Yes, Mama, I love you, too."

Marion Jo went to tend to her other children as Laurie Jo drank her milk and ate the brownies her mother had prepared.

Vickie and Nathaniel, Laurie Jo's baby sister and brother, were in the living room with the TV on. Vickie sat in front of it, engrossed by the cartoons. She was four years old, with a heart-shaped face, watery blue eyes, a button nose, and rosebud lips. Her hair was ash blonde and wavy and hung loosely down to her shoulders. She was wearing a white dress with pink daisies on it. Nathaniel was a chunky baby of one and a half years. He stood up in his playpen with a rattle in his mouth, his eyes wandering around, gazing at his oldest sister.

Laurie Jo enjoyed being their big sister. She always helped her mother with their care. She would play with them and giggled in their faces, and they would smile back at her. She held and fed them and gave them baths. She was incredibly careful and made sure they were handled with loving care. She was not like other older children, who usually resented a new sibling, acted out for attention, and were often jealous, feeling replaced or cheated out of their parents' love.

She did not physically resemble her siblings, for she had long, straight, reddish-brown hair. Her eyes, large and wide, were a deep, dark brown that sparkled as her mother's did. Her nose was pointed. Her lips were perky. This did not bother her, for she adored her baby brother and sister, immensely and dearly.

Marion Jo happened to be movie-star attractive. She had thick, wavy, blonde hair, with tendrils hanging down the sides of her face, always done and piled on her head, making her look older than her age. She free-lanced as a writer for a woman's magazine that she enjoyed immensely. She had the opportunities to meet interesting and worldly people, which made her gregarious and personable. Everyone loved her.

Kevin, her husband and her children's father, was a quiet but kind and gentleman, slow to anger and mild-mannered. He was the proprietor of a small textile business, which kept him busy a lot. However, he made every effort to be a family-oriented man. He had rustic, wavy hair, small blue eyes, a pudgy nose, and thick lips.

Kevin and Marion Jo loved each other, despite their personality polarities. As the saying goes, opposites attract. They were not openly physical, but they were deeply devoted to each other, and were good parents to their three children. They loved them unconditionally. The family stood by each other through thick and thin, supporting each other. They were a happy family.

Marion Jo stood by her living room window the next morning, watching her daughter head on the bus dressed in a short, puffed-sleeved white blouse with a thin white cardigan over it. She was wearing a red floral, knee-length skirt. On her feet were pastel-colored sneakers. Her long, dark hair was put in a bun with a red scrunchie around it. Curled tendrils hung down the sides of her face. Marion Jo sighed a pleasant sigh. For now, her daughter had friends. Before Laurie Jo left, she turned toward her mother after a hug and kiss and gleefully stated, "I love you, Mama!"

Marion Jo responded, "Me, too."

Laurie Jo was on her way to school, with happiness and joy!

3PM

At the end of the day, Laurie Jo waved to Anita and Suzanne, saying, "See you later, guys!" The two girls gave her a thumbs-up.

Mrs. Harrington took Laurie Jo's hand, leading her to an office down the hallway. Marion Jo was waiting for them. After they sat down, a tall, thin man with wire-frame glasses surrounding his small, light blue eyes, with receding hair, approached and greeted them.

"I'm Dr. Colmes." He extended his hand to each woman, and to Laurie Jo, who reciprocated with a smile. With his hand, he pointed to his office, ushering them in.

When they were seated, Dr. Colmes explained the situation. He looked at Laurie Jo, assuring her that he specialized in children's special needs and challenges. His job was to give a battery of tests to children to find out what issues they faced, and to find a suitable treatment plan for them.

He turned to Laurie Jo and asked her to make herself comfortable and secure, then posed her questions. He reassured her that she was not in any trouble and had not done anything wrong.

"Do you understand, Laurie Jo? You did nothing bad."

She nodded but remained silent.

"Can you tell me why you think you are here? Do not be afraid. We are all here to help you."

"Mrs. Harrington says I have trouble with reading and writing assignments."

Marion Jo chimed in, stating, "She always did, but all her former teachers did and said nothing, and just passed her along. Nothing was mentioned or pointed out. I was never informed of any problems she was having. I guess they just felt like passing her to the next grade. I tried to work with her at home. She tried, but still struggled. Then I hired a tutor, who practically agreed with me."

Dr. Colmes nodded slightly, tapping his pen on his desk. "I see." He understood.

Dr. Colmes turned to Mrs. Harrington and inquired of her, "What made you decide to seek help for Laurie Jo now, after all this time?"

Mrs. Harrington replied without hesitation, "Laurie Jo always struggled with anything involving reading and writing. I saw it a lot. I would ask her if she was all right, and she always insisted that she was. I knew she was just saying that because she was afraid of causing trouble and did not want to create any problems or difficulties. But I knew she was not—and she did, as well. To be frank, I should have found appropriate help for her earlier. I am sorry I did not. Please forgive me; I was wrong. But now, I have finally taken a stand. Most important, as you are already aware, there was a commotion in my class yesterday that made me realize my misjudgment in finding her support. I left the class for a meeting. My two honor students were put in charge. It was their responsibility to make sure the class behaved, and to report any problems. You see, the minute I went out, the students tormented Laurie Jo viciously, thinking it was funny. Anita and Suzanne tried to get them to stop but were unable to. Anita went to fetch me, explaining the situation. When I returned to the class, I shouted at them, while banging the hall pass on my desk. They all were punished."

Dr. Colmes listened attentively and patiently, with understanding.

Then he turned to Laurie Jo and asked her how she felt about what had occurred yesterday, and how she felt now.

Slowly, Laurie Jo started with great difficulty, in a low voice, sniffling, trying not to cry. She hiccupped and gulped uncontrollably, with her head down, hands on her lap.

"They wouldn't stop. They laughed and snickered at me." She could not resume.

Dr. Colmes assured her she was fine.

He added, "That must have been terrible and humiliating." He paused and continued, "How do you feel now?"

She raised her eyes, quietly affirming, without conviction: "Okay. I feel a little bit better."

"That's good." He was pleased.

"Now, young lady, I'll be taking you to a room down the corridor. I'll be administering a battery of tests to find out what your situation is, so I will be able to help you."

Laurie Jo inquired a little fearfully, "Will I be getting graded or yelled out if I don't know or can't do something?"

"No, absolutely not! Okay?" He reiterated, with great patience and tolerance. He wanted her to feel comfortable.

Then he arose from his chair and took her by her hand and led her to the examination room. Laurie Jo turned and waved to her mother and teacher. They smiled and nodded, assuring.

"We won't be long. Perhaps an hour or so," he informed them.

4:30PM

Dr. Colmes gathered all the papers together on his desk. Laurie Jo picked up her cardigan and backpack from the chair.

He turned toward her, instructing her, "That is all. I think everything is in order. Then to the woman standing by the door, he said, "Mrs. Boyle, would you please escort Laurie Jo to the cafeteria? I need to speak privately to Mrs. Harrington and Laurie Jo's mother, Mrs. Wentworth. Please have her back in about an hour."

Mrs. Boyle smiled at Laurie Jo and agreed: "Of course, Doctor."

Mrs. Boyle had been working as an aide at the school for over ten years. She had been married but, unfortunately, her husband had died unexpectedly, and they had been childless. She and her late husband were only children, so they had no nieces or nephews, either. Mrs. Boyle was very lonely, and she loved children dearly. She was loved by all the students and was like a second mother to them. She considered them her children and loved them as if they were her own. And in her mind, they were, even though she knew they were other peoples' children. She loved them and requested that they called her by her first name, though children were always told calling an adult by their first name was not respectful. She did not care. She always helped a student in trouble and listened to their problems with love and kindness, without judgment. She would offer them a snack, hold their hand, pat them on the back, or give them a hug when they were upset or unhappy. She never raised her voice or said an unpleasant word to any student, even the challenging ones.

Mrs. Boyle was a very plain woman but had a pleasant disposition. She wore owlish eyeglasses that framed her non-descript eyes. Her face was pale and colorless. Her hair was short and dish-watery blonde, styled in a bob. She wore a gray sweater over her plain tailored blouse. She had on a greenish-gray pleated skirt. On her feet, were flat, slip-on Oxford shoes.

Mrs. Boyle took Laurie Jo's hand. As they walked down the corridor, Mrs. Boyle lovingly complemented Laurie Jo as she looked at her with a smile, "Your hair is so pretty, and your skirt is glowing with colors!"

Then she asked, "Would you like some ice cream?"

Laurie Jo thanked her shyly for her compliments and then answered, "Yes, ma'am."

"Call me Irma, honey, okay? All the students do."

Laurie Jo looked up at her with a bright smile. "Irma." She addressed the woman gleefully and agreeably.

They resumed their walk to the cafeteria.

Dr. Colmes went down to the hallway, "Mrs. Harrington, Mrs. Wentworth—would you both please come down to my office? I assure you nothing is wrong. Laurie Jo isn't in any trouble."

He led them into his office and offered them seats in front of his desk.

"Laurie Jo is a sweet, bright, quiet child who tries and aims extremely hard to do what is expected of her. Her goal is to please people—especially you, Mrs. Wentworth. During the tests, Laurie Jo answered questions derived from stories and pictures I presented to her. She did not miss a single question; she received a perfect score. She even went on further with her answers, which were more than sufficient. She gets overly involved and eager. So, we could rule out her being mentally challenged. We could say she is extremely bright and gifted for someone of her age. However," he paused, "She was unable to match pictures of letters and numbers. She could not decipher them or put them in proper sequence. I asked her to write the letters and numbers I recited to her, but she struggled in her seat, erasing and crossing things out furiously while ripping the pages. She did know the letters and their sounds, but when I gave her a letter and its sound, she was flustered and shook uncontrollably. Tears formed in her eyes. Then I gently patted her hand to soothe her. I said, 'It's all right, Laurie Jo.' She stopped, looked up in pain, and apologized. I told her she had no reason to be upset or worried. I did ask her if she saw the letters and numbers jumping around on the page or if they were jumbled up in her mind. Right away, she sullenly nodded her head. I told her what the diagnosis was and that she did nothing wrong and she could be helped. We have a special label for this situation. Lots of people, mostly very bright people have it. Throughout the years, no one really understood or had a name for it. Thus, it went unnoticed and untreated. Nothing was ever done. Fortunately, that is no longer the case. Laurie Jo has dyslexia. I explained all of this to her. She seemed very composed and relieved."

Mrs. Boyle knocked on the door and entered, "We're back now, Doctor. Laurie Jo is a lovely girl," she said sincerely, "and very bright." She smiled at her.

"Thank you," he told her. "You can go now."

And to Laurie Jo, he pointed to a chair near her mother. "Please sit down next to your mother. Remember what we discussed before?"

"Yes," she replied softly, with a small but perky smile on her face, her eyes twinkling.

"You'll be going to a resource room for two hours every afternoon for help. Mr. Robinson will be your teacher. There will be three other students in the class. I called him, and he is expecting you tomorrow. Okay?"

Then he looked at her teacher and mother. "That will be all, ladies. It was a pleasure to meet you, Mrs. Wentworth. Laurie Jo is extremely fortunate to have you as her mother." And to Mrs. Harrington, he said, "You're a wonderful teacher."

Both ladies rose from their seats.

Mrs. Wentworth extended her hand and remarked positively, "Thank you so much for helping my daughter. You're a very wonderful and kind person."

Then she faced Mrs. Harrington and brightly thanked her: "And you, too, for your support, sensitivity, and kindness to my daughter. She is incredibly lucky to have you as her teacher. Laurie Jo speaks very highly of you."

Dr. Colmes concluded the meeting, "Have a good rest of the day, ladies." He returned to his desk.

Both ladies faced each other, shaking hands eagerly. Mrs. Harrington nodded at Laurie Jo, with sparkles in her eyes. "I'll see you in class tomorrow."

Laurie Jo beamed at her teacher.

"Let's go, honey." Mrs. Wentworth took her daughter's hand gently. Hand in hand, they left the office.

Mother and daughter swung their arms back and forth. Then, they hugged and kissed and joyfully shouted to each other by their car, not caring who was watching: "I love you all the way to Pluto and back!"

"My darling daughter of my heart," Marion Jo said proudly. People stared, but they paid them no heed.

"We're having your favorite tonight," Marion stated excitedly, "Spaghetti and meatballs!"

"Cool!" Laurie Jo exclaimed with joy.

"Oh, Mama," she continued, "Anita and Suzanne invited me to go to the movies this Saturday. May I—Mama, may I go?" She was breathless, jumping up and down in her seat.

"I don't see why not. But we must discuss it with Daddy. Okay, sweetheart?" she consented gently but firmly.

"You've never been anywhere without me and Daddy. I do trust you, but we'll have a meeting after dinner tonight, okay?"

"Oh, Mama!" Laurie sprang up with joy throwing her arms around her mother's neck with a peck on her cheek. "Oh, thank you. Thank you! I love you all the way to Pluto and back." She joyfully reiterated to her mother with love.

Marion Jo smiled and laughed excitedly, while keeping her eyes on the road.

"OK, OK, honey!" she affirmed, still with pleasure. Then she said to her daughter, "Me, too!"

They resumed the ride home, both extremely elated and content—smiles on their faces, gleaming stars twinkling in their eyes.

It was, indeed, an incredibly good day.

OH, DAUGHTER OF MINE, DAUGHTER OF MY HEART

Heloise – The mother – standing tall and erect, her jet-black, thick hair with peppery streaks, styled in waves below her ears; her large, dark, sharp, icy eyes piercing; lips, thick and wide, with no trace of a loving smile or a sweet, gentle demeanor—instead, a fiery, glaring, vicious disposition—as beautiful as a movie star, but vain, arrogant, and deceitful.

Olivia Crystal – The elder daughter – a plain but pleasant girl, her long, straight hair straw-like and colorless; her face wan and dry; without a sparkle or gleam in her watery, light brown eyes; brilliant in school, the top of her class. Some girlfriends, very little interest in boys.

Rhonda Gail – The younger daughter – with a heart-shaped face; large, bright, deep blue eyes gleaming as captive stars; a perky nose; perfectly shaped lips; her long blonde hair in waves; loving a different boy every week; not a determined, serious student—always cutting classes, taking off whenever she pleased, without respect for rules or authority.

Ronald – The father – not as bad—but no bargain; nothing special to brag about; callous, apathetic, completely oblivious to his environment, slow to anger; with a plain and non-descript face, large round blue eyes, a pot belly, a receding hair line.

I watched them, observing them from afar, in the background. They did not realize that I saw every move they made, and heard every word they uttered, as I muttered angrily to myself, with contempt.

The family sat around the kitchen table just finishing supper. Giggling with delight, Rhonda Gail spoke of her boyfriend — "the one," she proclaimed. Heloise, smiling sweetly, listened to her. Ronald hardly said anything, but sat in his chair, interested. Olivia Crystal got out of her chair, announcing she had a term paper to write.

Heloise turned and glared at her with arrogant contempt. "Do the dishes right now, young lady!"

Olivia Crystal quietly stated, "I did them last night. It's Rhonda Gail's turn."

Heloise paid her no heed and stood up, pointing her index finger while glaring contemptuously at her daughter. "I said, do them now—and not another word. I will not stand for such impertinence. If you refuse, you will be deeply sorry."

Olivia Crystal, standing rigidly, said nothing, unable to respond to her mother's vile demeanor. She nodded slowly, then left the table and washed the dishes in silence.

Rhonda Gail snickered under her breath watching. Ronald looked, but did not say a word. Heloise then smiled adoringly at her younger daughter and said, "Go on, dear."

After Olivia Crystal did the dishes, she went upstairs to her bedroom to work on her term paper, trying to stifle her sobbing. Her mother always favored her younger daughter. It had always been that way since they were children. Her parents gave Rhonda Gail everything she asked for. She did not have to work for what she demanded. They gave it to her with love. Especially her mother. Rhonda Gail wheedled, cajoled, pleaded, and whined. She was her mother's darling. She doted on her, though she willingly lied and made trouble. Olivia Crystal got blamed and scapegoated for all her misdeeds. Heloise hardly ever physically abused her—just emotionally, with cutting, biting words—and by denying her privileges. After a while, Olivia Crystal did not cry or scream violently, as she had when she had been younger. Helpless, she had learned that it was useless to fight back. She would give in and accept whatever it was.

She threw herself into her studies, dreaming of a better life—hoping, one day, that an elderly woman would love her for herself and take her to her heart. This is all she had to live for—to hold on to. She shared this with no one. It was her secret—hers and hers alone. No one could deny her this pleasure. She would smile with glee, feeling as though she were floating on air.

Suddenly, her bedroom door flew open, banging against the wall. It was her mother, with her hands on her hips, standing stoutly, her eyes blazing.

"Dry those dishes now. How dare you not do your chores!"

Quietly, struggling to suppress the tears brimming in her eyes, pleadingly and helplessly, knowing it was useless to defend herself, she managed to protest: "I washed them as you asked. It was Rhonda Gail's turn to dry."

Heloise ignored her remark. "Rhonda Gail said she washed them. Are you calling her a liar?"

Then Olivia Crystal bawled, her body shaking, "I'm innocent, I swear!! You know I am!"

Heloise smacked her face.

"Don't you dare raise your voice to me. And don't you ever lie to me—you ungrateful, spoiled little brat!" Then, she pointed to the door and, grabbing her daughter's arm, shoved her out to the top of the stairs. Olivia Crystal still sobbed uncontrollably.

"I want those dishes dried now. And I do not want to hear another word out of your mouth," she ordered, glaring at her daughter.

With a mournful, pained look on her face, speechless, she complied.

TWO MONTHS LATER – GRADUATION DAY

Olivia Crystal was valedictorian of her graduating class. It was her day, a good day. Nothing to spoil it. She never told her parents or sister about this day. It was hers and hers alone. After the ceremony, she went with her girlfriends to the Shake Shop. They sat around, laughing and chattering away. She knew her family would not be there to celebrate with her so she resigned herself to that fate. She had plans.

When she arrived home, she packed all her belongings. One friend offered to let her stay at her house until she got a job. She intended to go to college in the fall to major in library sciences, since she loved books, and read voraciously.

She left home, leaving her wretched childhood behind. And she never looked back or returned. Her new life began. She was in heaven.

I had been watching and observing them from afar in the background. I was Olivia Crystal's guardian angel. She needed my help desperately, and I was determined to give it to her.

Witnessing these explosive, heart-wrenching dramas, I gritted my teeth, irate, burning and seething with anger, attempting to hold my fiery temper. I visualized myself hurling vile, bitter expletives at her mother.

"How dare you, you fuckin' cunt! How dare you!" I would scream, with fright in my voice. My eyes piercing red, afire, I would shout, "You fuckin' cunt!" My body would be shaking. "Don't you ever make my mother look like Josephine! You hear me?!" I would yell in her face. "You are going to pay for how you treated Olivia Crystal. She is a wonderful, nice person." I would stress, refusing to back down or cave in.

"I'm not through with you yet, you motherfuckin' bitch! You will be sorry. Mark my words." Then, calmly, I staunchly added, "What goes around comes around."

The mother would look at me with fright. She would be terrified of me. She would be unable to utter a word. "What the hell is wrong with you?! Stop harassing me or I will call 911, and they will cart you away to a place for crazies like you!"

I would laugh hysterically at this evil, vicious woman of ill repute. She would have nothing on me. She would know she was defeated. Sullenly, with her head down, she would turn and walked away. I would triumph, smiling, and turn my head up to the clear blue sky, the sun's rays beaming down on me. I won the war.

TWENTY-FIVE YEARS LATER

I had been secretly watching Olivia Crystal during these past years. She filled out, becoming quite attractive—the ugly duckling turned into a beautiful swan. Her long, thick, straight hair was brown as the earth, and hung down on her shoulders. Her eyes glistened. Her lips were curvy. Her face was bright and colorful, no longer pale or wan.

She had graduated from college with a master's in library sciences, fulfilling her dream to become a librarian. She was an exceptionally good one. Everyone loved her, for she was always kind, helpful, obliging, and patient. Her biography appeared in many Who's Who of America Editions. She never married, for she never loved a man so much that she would want to spend her life with him. She knew it would not be fair for him or for her. Also, a wish for an elderly woman's unconditional love did come about. She bonded with several such women, who encouraged her to believe in herself and tried to convince her that she was special, sweet, and kind. But she knew and understood they had their own lives.

She did have some girlfriends. However, most of them married and started their own families. They would exchange birthday and greeting cards. She would email them and vice versa with news, but that was it. She was satisfied with her life. She did suffer from a psychiatric illness and saw a psychiatrist regularly who prescribed medication for her nerves. She enrolled in options classes at the local college and attended workshops, events, and seminars at the JCC, where she met other people. The JCC organized excursions, such as boat rides, shows, museums, and out-of-town trips. She seemed to be content, doing well and moving on with her life. I was happy for her. But, deep down, I knew the hurt and pain from her abusive childhood reigned over her.

I then stepped in and took control. All these years, she did not know I was watching over her, praying for her. She did not know I was concerned for her emotional and mental well-being. I decided to come forth.

One evening, I saw her in her condominium, typing on her laptop keyboard. I stood by her window. I felt uneasy. How could I help her? Would she think I was stalking and harassing her? I hoped she would not. I wanted to be with and help her. I needed to convince her of my good intentions. I decided to seize this opportunity. I would persevere until I accomplished my goal to help her heal and find peace. I was finally going to reveal my identity to her.

Hesitantly, I rapped on the door. A few seconds later, she appeared. She was not anxious or fearful, but she was not gleeful either. She was awed and puzzled, just standing there, saying nothing at first. I approached her, making sure she would not be afraid, thinking I would harm her.

"I don't know how to begin, and you might think I'm a nut job. And I wouldn't blame you," I began, choosing my words carefully, with kindness and gentleness. She continued to stand still, silently gazing at me. "I want you to know I've been observing you most of your life. You were never aware of it. But," I put my hand up, "I am your guardian angel. I swear, I have no malicious intentions. My motives are completely altruistic. I want to help you. I saw how your family, especially your mother, treated you." I paused again. Still, she said not a word, but did not seem afraid. But she was bewildered and a bit surprised. A few seconds later, she seemed comfortable and at ease.

Finally, she quietly offered, "Come in. I will make us tea. Please, sit down," she ushered me toward her kitchen table.

When we were finally seated and at ease with each other, I resumed what I had originally intended to suggest.

"I know you were severely abused by your mother. She was wrong. But I think you are still letting it hover over your head, preventing you from being happy. Though I am aware you have managed to go on with your life and fulfill your dreams, I still strongly suggest you forgive her by writing a letter. I know that you vowed to never look back at those times where you experienced such pain and hurt. But the worst that can happen is that she will either not acknowledge you or own up to her behavior toward you in the past. But you need to come full circle. Do not let this torment or keep you from having and living the kind of life you deserve. Also, do not let it fester and build up in your mind anymore. I hope you understand, okay?"

Olivia Crystal nodded solemnly. Finally, she smiled agreeably, though hesitantly.

"You're right, I should," she admitted, "I'll do it first thing tomorrow morning." Afterward, she extended her hand to me, leading me through her condominium. I saw she had a bedroom and another room she called her office. I saw mountains of books and magazines all throughout her condo.

An hour later, I left, bidding her 'goodbye'. Likewise, she did, too.

THE NEXT MORNING, 8AM

Sitting at her laptop, Olivia Crystal began:

"Dear Mother, . . ."

She was nervous, but eager.

TWO MONTHS LATER

I received her email. All it said was, "I did it. Please come over. I have a lot to tell you." No sign of anger or bitterness, just an eagerness to share.

I left, jumping on the bus. Anxiously awaiting the news. Whatever it was. I wanted to know. Not for me, but for her.

I arrived, knocking gingerly, anxiously, at her door.

Olivia Crystal appeared, opening her door. She was in a cheerful mood. I was incredibly happy for her.

As we sat down, she began: "She actually acknowledged me. I thought she would yell or scream, hurling hateful words at me, like she did when I was a little girl. She did not. She called me a week after she received my letter. She wanted to see me. Really! We planned to meet for lunch this Saturday. She said we would talk and attend counselling sessions. She said that! I could not believe it. I would have been satisfied if she had not responded. But she did more than I could ever have imagined. She sounded as though she was apologizing. But I do not want to get my hopes up. I, really, really did not expect any of this. Really!"

I was joyful for her. Even if she did not get a reply or if her mother were still abusive, I would have been happy for her anyway. Because she had taken a stand—a chance—without any guarantees. She could move on now.

"I'm incredibly happy for you, Olivia Crystal. And good luck this Saturday. I'll be watching you, all right?"

She replied in the affirmative.

SATURDAY, 1PM

Olivia Crystal was dressed in a long, puffed-sleeved, red floral peasant blouse and a red gypsy skirt that swayed as she walked. She wore open-toe, sling-back sandals. She had a beaded necklace on her neck and bracelets on her wrists. Pearl string earrings hung down from her lobes.

She saw her. The woman who gave her life and was supposed to love her unconditionally, not abuse her. She had aged, no longer the raving beauty she once had been. Life had taken a toll on her. She was barely sixty years old but looked eighty-five. Her face sagged, her hair was unruly, with gray streaks, her deadpan eyes were tired and weary. Her hands were wrinkled and had varicose veins. She wore a tattered gray coat. Her leather slip-on shoes were too big for her feet, making her shuffle uneasily. She had a ragged, colorless hat skewed on her head.

She looked up at her daughter, saying nothing at first. She just stared at her, showing no emotion. But she wanted to. She just could not now. Olivia Crystal did not know how to begin. Both stood like statues facing each other wordlessly in the street.

Finally, Olivia Crystal addressed her shyly: "Mother?"

Then Heloise burst into loud weeping, crying uncontrollably, tears flowing down her face.

Olivia Crystal wanted to run up to her, to hug and kiss her, as she always had wanted to do when she had been a little girl fiercely hungry for her mother's love.

"I'm sorry, so sorry!" She bawled.

Surprisingly, Heloise put out her hands to her daughter. She did not jump away, but cried, also. Suddenly, they embraced as though it was second nature for them. They held each other for a long while, weeping, their hearts breaking. People stared, but they did not mind. Tears streamed down their faces, their eyes red and puffy. As they released each other, Heloise held out her hand to her daughter, "Come, come to Mother, darling," she struggled with the words. Olivia Crystal took her mother's hand and entered the restaurant.

They sat down at a table, facing each other mournfully. Again, Heloise took her daughter's hands in hers, patting then softly. Though she was surprised at her mother's gesture Olivia Crystal did not pull away.

A waiter came up to them with a courteous smile and asked, "Are you ladies ready to order?"

Olivia Crystal answered, "Please, give us a few minutes. We should be ready shortly."

He agreeably bowed his head and left.

Heloise fidgeted with the glass of water in front of her, her eyes on the menu, not facing her daughter, who put her hand in hers.

"It's all right. I'm okay."

"You didn't deserve any of my abusiveness. You were always a good daughter. I never told you that while you were growing up and I am deeply ashamed of myself."

Olivia Crystal listened attentively to her mother's words but was not able to respond at first. It was a lot to take in.

Hesitantly, Heloise went on, but stuttered on her words, unable to enunciate clearly. Her thoughts, muddled and garbled. The tears arose again, but this time she managed to blurt out without pausing to catch her breath.

"Ronald is not your father," she said flatly and matter-of-factly. "Before I married him, I was raped by a neighborhood boy while I was going home from school. I was sixteen years old. The boy dragged me by the hair into the woods. He stripped my clothes off and put it in me forcibly before I could do or say anything. It hurt like hell, but I was too scared to scream out for help. I laid there like a rag doll. Then, I discovered I was pregnant with you. I wanted to abort you because I had no support, guidance, or love from my own parents—especially my mother. They had me marry Ronald, a local boy whose parents they knew and liked very much. They said Ronald was a decent boy who was willing to make me respectful. It did not matter that we did not love each other—he was a good provider, and responsible. He was willing to support me and you. My parents demanded that I keep you, because they did not believe in abortion back then and said you were my punishment. They blamed me, and the boy was let off the hook. Nothing was ever said about or done to him. You looked exactly like him." She put her head down in her hands, struggling to catch her breath.

Olivia Crystal stared at her mother. She understood and believed she was sorry. She was. But, still, she had not uttered a word for a while.

"I forgive you," she held out her hand, patting her mother's hand with affection.

Heloise went on. "I'm so proud of you. You have accomplished quite a bit in your life and happen to be highly intelligent. You have quite a fine mind. Most of all, you are beautiful. I know I said you physically resembled the boy who forced himself upon me. That was not right. You are a very pretty and sweet young lady, and I'm honored to be your mother and have you as my daughter."

Olivia Crystal quipped up. "What about Rhonda Gail? How is she doing now?" She was very curious and interested in the half-sister who had been deeply loved, knowing she had not at all been a pleasure or joy to her parents.

Heloise glanced at the glass she had in her hand, replying with sadness and regret.

"I loved her. But she did not deserve my love. She was a brat—ill-natured and spoiled. She slept around with boys, cut school, dealt drugs, stole, and habitually lied to me. She would go off for days. I would be worried sick, but it did not faze her. She has been in constant trouble with the law and was arrested for prostitution, armed robbery, and drug possession and drug dealing. She thought it was all a big joke, and would laugh raucously in my face, assuming I would be there to clean up her messes, time and time again. She had no respect for me and would curse in my face. Thus, I finally decided to end it once in for all. I told her I had had enough picking up the pieces and had her committed to a psychiatric facility permanently. She could not understand since I have always been bailing her out and forgiving her. Not anymore. I do visit her occasionally, for she is my daughter. But you are my daughter, and I did not do right by you. I was sexually assaulted, and I took it out on you. It was not your fault. I was raped and you were the product of a bad seed. But you are not a bad seed. No one helped or supported me. Believe it or not, I am glad I did not abort you. Sometimes, beauty and loveliness arise from dirt, trash, and ugliness. You were and are so very lovely, to this day."

Olivia Crystal continuing to stare at her mother, listening to her heart-wrenching life. She felt pity and sorrow for her, despite the cruel and harsh treatment she had received. She wanted to understand. And, more importantly, she wanted to forgive, which they both know would take time.

Olivia Crystal asked about the man she had, for all these years, thought had been her father but had just found out was not.

Heloise fumbled with the glass in her hands, her eyes bowed, and answered her daughter's request sadly.

"He's in a rest home. He has dementia and does not even know who I am anymore. He knew you were not his biological daughter. Though he was not abusive to you, he neglected you. He did not realize how hurt you were. So, please, do no blame him. I am the one deserving of blame. I hurt you very badly and I know it will be hard for you to forgive me but, hopefully, in time, you will. I want to be your mother, always and forever. I want to be there for you, and support you through thick and thin. I want to get to know all about you. As you know, I suggested counselling for us. I feel it will help us mend our relationship. Too much time has gone by and been wasted. I want to start over. I do not blame you if you hate me or think I don't deserve your love. You do have a right to that, and I want to give it to you before it's too late, all right?" she pleaded.

"I don't hate you. And I do forgive you. And," Olivia Crystal paused, spreading her hands on the table, struggling and gasping for air. "I love you," she affirmed staunchly and sincerely. Though she did not look at her mother, she added, slowly but with love, "Mama!"

Heloise cried aloud, with a gleam in her eyes, and a small, slight smile. "I love you, too, oh, daughter of mine, daughter of my heart."

With big, bright smiles on their faces, eyes lively and shiny, they picked up their menus to decide what to order.

I watched them for the last time. Mother and daughter. Loving, forever and always.

I was quite content. Incredibly happy, indeed. Olivia Crystal Wellington did not need my help anymore. She would be simply fine. My work was finished. With a smile on my face, my eyes glistening, feeling very, very pleased, and breathing in the fresh air, I turned and walked away, gazing up at the sun shining brightly from the clear blue sky, which glowed on my face.

It was indeed an incredibly good day. Everything was exactly as it was supposed to be—good and wonderful. I sighed gleefully.

MY OWN TRUE PERSONAL ACCOUNT

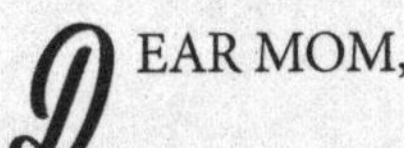

EAR MOM,

M is for magnanimous, mellifluous, magnificent, marvelous, maternal.

O is for outstanding, open, overt, obvious.

T is for titillating, thrilling, tender, true, trustworthy.

H is for happy, hopeful, helpful, heartwarming.

E is for exhilarating, enthusiastic, earthy, exciting, effusive, emollient, enlightening, extolling, extraverted, exuberant.

R is for ravishing, righteous, revealing, rapturous.

LOVE ALWAYS,
YOUR LOVING, DARLING DAUGHTER,
BETH CAROL

INCIDENT IN THE SUMMER OF 1961

I SAW THEM –

THE MOTHER-

THE DAUGHTER –

FROM THE BACKS OF THEIR HEADS

COMPLETELY OBLIVIOUS TO ME

STRANGERS

THE MOTHER –

TALL AND SLIM

WITH SHORT, LIGHT BROWN, WAVY HAIR, NEATLY STYLED

WEARING A HAT

DRESSED AS ONE GOING TO THE PRESIDENT'S BALL

THE DAUGHTER –

ABOUT SEVEN YEARS OLD

PLUMP AND PLAIN

WITH DEADPAN EYES

PALE AS A GHOST

WEARING A LIGHT BLUE DRESS

HAIR – STRAIGHT, MOUSY BROWN, PULLED BACK IN A PONYTAIL

THE MOTHER – ARROGANT AND A WOMAN OF ILL REPUTE

GLARING AT HER WITH FIERY BLACK EYES

A LOOK THAT COULD SPLIT ROCK

FOR NO REASON, SMACKED HER DAUGHTER ON HER BEHIND

GRABBING HER HAND, SAYING SEDUCTIVELY AND IN A NASTY TONE,

"GIVE ME YOUR HAND!"

THE DAUGHTER – INNOCENT AND TIMID, QUIET AS A MOUSE, HELPLESS AND POWERLESS, DOING ABSOLUTELY NOTHING WRONG, STOOD THERE, TAKING HER MOTHER'S UNJUSTIFIABLE ABUSE PASSIVELY, LIKE A CATATONIC MENTAL PATIENT, A SPHINX, A STATUE, STONE-FACED, DEVOID OF

EMOTION AND EXPRESSION

THIS INCIDENT-

TAKING A FRACTION OF A SECOND

BUT – I

SCREAMING AFTERWARD, INSIDE MYSELF, CONTINUALLY FOR YEARS,

AT THE MOTHER IN A FURIOUS BURNING RAGE-

"HOW DARE YOU MAKE MY MOTHER LOOK LIKE JOSEPHINE!"

YOU MOTHER FUCKING CUNT-FACE BITCH!!!"

QUICKLY, SHE TURNS TOWARD ME IN AGHAST AND SAYS

HER EYES BOLTING OUT OF THEIR SOCKETS

"WHAT THE HELL IS WRONG WITH YOU?

YOU'RE CRAZY!

YOU KNOW THAT?!

STOP HARASSING ME OR I'LL CALL THE POLICE AND HAVE THEM CART YOU AWAY TO AN INSANE

ASYLUM!"

I, THEN, LAUGH AND SAY WITHOUT CONVICTION OR JUSTIFICATION.

“MAKING MY MOTHER LOOK LIKE JOSEPHINE ISN'T AN OPTION!”

I FEEL NO REMORSE AND DO NOT APOLOGIZE.

WHY SHOULD I?

I HAVE EVERY RIGHT TO BE ANGRY.

SHE IS WRONG.

“YOU HAD NO RIGHT ABUSING YOUR DAUGHTER IN A PUBLIC PLACE. SHE DID NOTHING WRONG.”

SHE IS STILL STANDING THERE DUMBFOUNDEDLY AND COMPLETELY SPEECHLESS

I WALK AWAY QUIETLY, MY BIG DARK BROWN EYES AS GLEAMING STARS SPARKLING

SMILING TO MYSELF

FEELING VERY, VERY HAPPY, SATISFIED, AND GLEEFUL.

I DID WHAT I HAD TO DO

WITHOUT ANY SIGN OF SORROW OR REMORSE

DANCING ON AIR

IN LOVE WITH LOVE

IN LOVE WITH LIFE

TODAY IS A SIMPLY WONDERFUL DAY FOR ME FOREVER

I GAZE UP AT THE SKY

THE SUN SHINING BRIGHTLY

ALL IS WELL IN THE WORLD

AND ONE MORE THING—

JOSEPHINE, MY DARLING LADY LOVE

GOD REST YOUR SOUL

REST IN PEACE

I LOVE YOU FOREVER AND ALWAYS

FAST FORWARD MANY, MANY YEARS LATER

I THINK

"YOU HAVE MY COMPLETE FORGIVENESS,"

I SAY TO THAT MOTHER

SURROUNDING HER WITH A GLOWING LIGHT

"FOR WHAT YOU DID,

ASK NOW FOR GOD'S

AND BE AT PEACE."

ALSO, FOR SOME STRANGE REASON I COULDN'T FATHOM AT THAT TIME, BUT NOW I DO.

"I WISH YOU WELL

WHO AND WHEREVER YOU ARE.

YOU GO YOUR WAY

AND I'LL GO MINE.

GOD BLESS YOU

AND MORE IMPORTANTLY,

BELIEVE IT OR NOT,

YOUR DAUGHTER LOVES YOU VERY MUCH INSPITE OF EVERYTHING.

SHE HAS THE RIGHT TO BE LOVED BY YOU UNCONDITIONALLY."

THEN AFTERWARD—

WHILE LOOKING UP AT THE HEAVENLY SKY

I SEE JOSEPHINE

WHO NEVER HAD A MEAN OR BAD THOUGHT

FOR ANYONE

NO MATTER THE CIRCUMSTANCES

AND WHO ALWAYS ENCOURAGED LOVE AND FORGIVENESS,

WINKS AT ME WITH A GLEAM IN HER EYES,

SMILING AT ME LOVINGLY

I SMILE BACK

THANK YOU, DEAREST JO, FOR SHOWING ME THE WAY

PART TWO

The Clock Family

THE CLOCKS: PORTRAIT OF A HAPPY FAMILY

THERE THEY ARE

IN THE CAR

ALL SMILING FACES

GAZING AT THE CLEAR BLUE SUNNY SKY

THE FATHER – A GOOD AND WONDERFUL FAMILY MAN

ALWAYS THERE FOR THEM THROUGH THICK AND THIN

MILD-MANNERED AND QUIET

THE MOTHER – WITH SHORT, WAVY RED HAIR,

WHO LOVES HER CHILDREN DEEPLY AND UNCONDITIONALLY,

A WARM AND LOVING LADY

BOTH – SLOW TO ANGER

COMPASSIONATE AND UNDERSTANDING WITH THEIR CHILDREN WHEN THEY ARE IN PAIN AND NEED COMFORT AND HELP

THE DAUGHTER – WITH BRIGHT, GLEAMING BLUE EYES AND SHOULDER-LENGTH, CURLY, LIGHT BROWN HAIR, SEVEN YEARS OLD, WITH A GIGGLY, PERKY, CHEEKY AND SASSY PERSONALITY, MAKES FRIENDS EASILY AND WITHOUT A CARE OR WORRY IN THE WORLD

THE SON – TWO YEARS OLDER THAN HIS SISTER, A GOOD BROTHER, CURIOUS ABOUT THE WORLD AROUND HIM, ALWAYS LOOKING FOR FUN AND A NEW ADVENTURE, ENJOYS COLLECTING BASEBALL CARDS AND STAMPS, AND 'LOVES TAKING CARE OF HIS PET HAMSTER

AT THE END OF THE DAY

THE FAMILY HUGS AND KISSES EACH OTHER WHILE SAYING GOODNIGHT

AND, MOST IMPORTANTLY, "I LOVE YOU TO THE MOON AND BACK!!!"

THE END OF ANOTHER GOOD DAY IN THE CLOCK FAMILY

YES, MY DARLING DAUGHTER

"MAMA, MAMA!" THE LITTLE GIRL CALLED JOYFULLY WHILE RUNNING INTO THE HOUSE, WAVING A PIECE OF PAPER OVER HER HEAD.

KATHERINE JOSEPHINE, WORKING AT THE COUNTER IN THE KITCHEN, TURNED AROUND AND SMILED GLEEFULLY. HER BEAUTIFUL, LARGE, BROWN EYES SPARKLING LIKE CAPTIVE STARS, SHE ASKED,

"YES, MY DARLING DAUGHTER?"

SHE WAVED THE PAPER AT HER MOTHER WHILE JUMPING UP AND DOWN AND AROUND AND AROUND. "LOOK, LOOK! I RECEIVED 100% ON OUR SOCIAL STUDIES EXAMINATION FOR MY GRADE. I WAS THE ONLY ONE WITH A PERFECT SCORE IN THE WHOLE SECOND GRADE. THE AWARDS CEREMONY WILL BE HELD THIS SATURDAY NIGHT IN THE ASSEMBLY. THE WHOLE SCHOOL WILL BE THERE."

KATHERINE JOSEPHINE TOOK THE PAPER AND STARED AT IT WITH MUCH JOY. "HOW WONDERFUL. OH, HONEY, I'M SO PROUD OF YOU! WAIT UNTIL I SHOW DADDY AND ANDREW. I THINK WE SHOULD CELEBRATE. HOW ABOUT US MAKING CHOCOLATE CHIP COOKIES TOGETHER? THOSE ARE THEIR FAVORITES.

OH, SUSIE, I'M SO PROUD OF YOU. BUT, YOU KNOW, I'M ALWAYS PROUD AND DO LOVE YOU NO MATTER WHAT YOU DO! YOU'RE A SWEET, SPECIAL, AND WONDERFUL LOVING LITTLE GIRL. I'M VERY HAPPY YOU'RE MY DAUGHTER. MY DARLING DAUGHTER!"

THEY HUGGED AND KISSED AS THEY DANCED AROUND AND AROUND, NEVER STOPPING, FLOATING ON AIR. A REAL, SPECIAL DAY. A SUNSHINY DAY FOREVER.

THEN, THEY TURNED TOWARD THE COUNTER, WORKING TOGETHER, SIDE BY SIDE, SMILING GLEEFULLY AT EACH OTHER, MAKING THE COOKIES

DINNER WITH THE CLOCK FAMILY

Katherine Josephine, clad in a blue floral house dress and a frilly lace apron, was singing and smiling to herself while she was preparing the finishing touches of the day's supper. She stirred the sauce in the pot with meatballs. She made sure the spaghetti was soft and creamy and checked the microwave to see if the frozen mixed vegetables were hot and ready. Another pot with rice was simmering. The baked potatoes were creamy and soft. She briefly looked at the clock above the stove. It read 3 P.M.

She heard cheerful voices outside in front of the house. She gazed out the window. Her children were getting off the school bus. They smiled and waved to the other children on the bus, who waved back.

"Bye, now," the little girl said.

"See you," her older brother stated.

"My darlings, my babies," Katherine Josephine smiled pleasantly and smugly to herself, her eyes wide and bright as captive stars.

The front door burst open. They dashed into the house, slipping off their backpacks and thrusting them aside.

Andrew, the son, who had straight, light brown hair was wearing a blue baseball cap, a long-sleeved plaid flannel shirt, and brown jeans.

Susie, who had shoulder length, tousled, mousy hair, nine years old, wore a short puffed-sleeved blouse with rosebuds embroidered on it; her sky-blue jacket was opened. Her blue denim jeans had flowers sewn on the bottom.

Both children were wearing white sneakers, their laces untied.

Their mother, with her arms wide open, asked, "Where are my hugs and kisses?"

Without batting an eye, Susie ran into her mother's arms giving her affection, "Mama! Mama! I love you all the way to Pluto and back!"

Andrew hesitated. He did love his mother, but at his age of eleven and a half, he felt a little embarrassed. But he proclaimed, "Hi, Mom!"

She was not insulted. She understood.

"Brownies and chocolate milk are on the table for you both. I know you two love brownies, so I made them especially for you. But, first, go wash your hands and face, okay?"

The children bounded upstairs, poking and nudging each other playfully while giggling.

"Be careful, you two," their mother instructed as she watched them protectively. Though she knew they were just being silly and that that was how children were, she still worried they would go too far and unintentionally get hurt.

TWO HOURS LATER

Katherine Josephine called upstairs, "Children! Daddy's home!"

First Susie, then Andrew flew down the stairs, running up to their father. Susie gave him a hug. He picked her up and swung her around in the middle of the living room. She was laughing.

"How's my favorite little girl?"

"Wonderful, just wonderful, Daddy," she replied gleefully.

Andrew smiled at his father and gave him a high five and a pat on the back.

"And how is my little man doing?"

"I've got a new video game." He showed his father the game, who glanced at it with interest.

"Let's check it out after supper, okay?"

Andrew grinned happily, "Oh, yes, yes, Dad."

Katherine Josephine walked up to her husband, and they kissed each other on the cheek.

She inquired to her husband, "How was your day, Edward Ferdinand?" as she gazed lovingly in his eyes.

"Can't complain," he replied flatly but with a smile. He always said that. Nothing really bothered him. He was easy-going and placid. Never saying or thinking negative thoughts. Very laidback, no matter the situation or circumstances.

"Dinner's almost ready," she said.

Turning to her daughter, she asked, "How about helping me serve dinner? It has been a long day."

Susie agreed with amity and without protest. She rose from her chair to help her mother.

HALF AN HOUR LATER

The Clock family were seated at the table waiting to be served.

"Anyone want a roll?" Katherine Josephine offered while passing around the basket.

The children shouted at once, digging into them hungrily.

"One at a time," instructed Katherine Josephine firmly but gently.

Edward Ferdinand, picking up his fork, dug into the meatballs and spaghetti. After putting it in his mouth and chewing ravenously, he complimented his wife brightly, "This is so delicious, honey."

Their children also dug into their plates, like their father, chewing their food with gusto.

"Way to go, Mom," Andrew glanced at his mother.

"Oh, my!" Susie lithely said while crunching her meatball with excitement, "Way to go, Mama!" she added.

Katherine Josephine was pleased. She looked at each family member, "It's such a pleasure, all I do for my appreciative family."

They resumed their meal, enjoying every bite of it. Everyone smiled at each other.

"Mom," Andrew faced his mother and suggested, "I have a great idea. Why don't each of us share a wonderful aspect of our day? In other words, let us talk about an event that occurred today we are each grateful for."

Edward Ferdinand gazed as his son in agreement. "Not a bad idea, son." He turned to his wife.

"Why not?" she agreed with contentment. She faced her daughter. "Why don't you begin?"

"All right," she said elatedly, "I received an A on my social studies. Ms. Marshall said it was the best one in the class! And that is not all. You know what, Mama, Daddy? The smartest and cutest boy in my class nominated me for class president," the little girl announced gingerly. "I think I sort of like him, perhaps he likes me, but it really doesn't matter, you know." She turned from her mother and then her father. Then, while wagging her index finger around to her parents, her eyes shining as captive stars, while jumping up and down in her seat, she went on with excitement, "Francesca invited me to her house for a sleepover."

Francesca had been Susie's best friend since kindergarten, along with another little girl, Alexandria. Katherine Josephine had been friends with her mother for over two years. They met in the supermarket and happened to be searching for the same laundry detergent. They got to talking and Alexandria's mother had asked Katherine Josephine to join her and three other women for a mahjong group that took place every Tuesday evening.

"Is it okay, Mama?" she begged earnestly to her mother, "Please, can I? I promise to be good and to do all my chores without being reminded. Can I? Can I?" she implored again.

"Of course, you may," she consented with a smile. "But we do have to make sure you are prepared for it. You have never been to one, so you will require essential instructions of what to do. I do trust you; you know that. But unforeseen situations can arise, so you must know what to do, okay?" She nodded agreeably at her daughter.

Susie jumped out of her chair, nearly knocking it over and threw her arms around her mother's neck nearly choking her, "Oh, Mama, thank you, thank you. I love you forever and ever." Katherine Josephine laughed and smiled while patting her on the back.

Then, toward her husband, she asked, "How about you, Edward Ferdinand?" She waited for his answer.

"According to most people, being a CPA is kind of a dull, boring, and nerdy job. But I look at it this way: people come to me for financial advice, and I can, most of the time, help them make wise choices. Sometimes, I am not able to. However, I am grateful to be of service, regardless. For those I cannot help, I try to think of other avenues and resources that might be available to serve their needs."

Andrew piped up, "Very interesting, Dad. Finding the good from what is presumed dull and boring. As for me, taking care of my hamster brings me joy and satisfaction. I get to take care of and be responsible for a pet—a living, breathing creation of God, who chose me for the path of helping animals. You know, people tend to take pets for granted. I don't."

"That's wonderful," his mother remarked proudly while glancing at each member of her family.

Then, Edward Ferdinand addressed his wife, "Now, my dear. How about your day?"

"Being a saleslady could be challenging and hard at times because customers can be frustrating. But if I can help someone make the right decision, what can I say? I am happy either way, so I treat everyone as an important individual. I smile and nod and thank them for coming into the store, and wish them a blessed day."

"Boy, Mom, that's really cool. I could never do what you do. I'm too impatient—especially with ungrateful, nasty people," Andrew pointed out.

Katherine Josephine worked in a small ladieswear boutique part time three days a week, four hours a day. She loved it. The family did not really need the extra income, since Edward Ferdinand's job paid excellent wages, with four weeks' vacation time, holiday bonuses, health insurance benefits, and a guaranteed annual salary increase. But she enjoyed working with people and had a very cheerful demeanor toward all the customers, no matter if they were rude, sullen, abrupt, or snippy. She treated everyone with kindness and respect. When she would wish them a good day, she meant it, while others would do it in an automatic, robotic style, with a grouchy attitude, because it was required of them. She never had an attitude. Everyone loved her, for she had a warm, kind heart.

TWO HOURS LATER

Susie and her mother cleared the table, stacked the dishes into the dishwasher, scrubbed the sink and wiped down the counters. Andrew and Edward Ferdinand went into the living room, switched on the television to a game show channel. They kept shouting with laughter while jumping up and down in front of the television, with their hands up in the air. Katherine Josephine and Susie watched them and laughed.

"They're so silly, Mama," Susie remarked matter-of-factly.

"Yes, they are," she agreed pleasantly.

"How about some popcorn, ladies?" Edward Ferdinand called out.

Both mother and daughter harmoniously replied, "Coming right up!"

After they finished cleaning up, they put the dish towels down on the counter, started the dishwasher, reached for a package of popcorn, and inserted it the microwave, waiting for it to be edible and crispy. It took three minutes.

"Here you go, boys, right out of the oven." After they took the bowl, they grabbed at it ravenously, still glued to the television.

"One at a time, please," Katherine Josephine gently ordered.

All four Clock family members were crunching and digging into the bowl, watching the nightly game shows. All smiling and laughing. Together. In harmony.

8:30PM

"Time for bed, children," Katherine Josephine instructed firmly, but lovingly.

"School tomorrow," their father chimed in.

Obediently, Susie and Andrew rose from the couch.

"Goodnight, Mom, Dad," Andrew agreeably responded, with a slight, pleasant smile.

Then, Susie chimed in, "Goodnight, Mama, Daddy," in her little girl voice.

"Where are my hugs and kisses?" Katherine Josephine asked, knowing quite well she and Edward Ferdinand would get loving reactions from their darling children.

"Mine, too?" Edward Ferdinand volunteered afterward.

They went to their mother, then to their father. "Love you both, all the way to Pluto and back!"

"Us, too," their parents reciprocated, with smiles and sparkles in their eyes.

The children bounded up the stairs, giggling and playfully jabbing each other in the ribs.

When they were in bed for the night, Edward Ferdinand turned to his wife, giving her a kiss on her cheek.

"Another wonderful day, honey."

"Yes," she affirmed sincerely. "It surely was."

Edward Ferdinand put his arms around his wife, she, leaning against his chest. She kissed him back.

They went back to the television, watching the game shows. All smiles, as they gazed dreamily at each other with love.

They were all truly blessed.

MOTHER'S DAY WITH THE CLOCK FAMILY

SUNDAY, 7 A.M.

Katherine Josephine was tossing and turning in bed, trying to cover her ears with a pillow. She had been trying to sleep for a while, but could not, due to the racket downstairs. She was not someone who got riled easily, but she was not a morning person, and just wanted to sleep in, for it was Sunday, a day of rest.

"What's going on?" she thought to herself. All she wanted was peace and quiet. And she was unable to because the noise downstairs was getting louder and unbearable. She heard the rattling and banging of objects in the kitchen. It went on and on. All she asked was to be able to sleep in, for she had no reason to get up. She had no plans. Just complete solitude.

Then, she heard loud voices—her family giving orders to each other that she could not decipher. Why were they making so much noise? Did they not realize she liked to sleep in on a Sunday morning, without any hassle? It was useless, she considered hopelessly. Her family was always considerate of her feelings. But not today, for some strange reason. She could not fathom it. The racket continued. It did not end. All she asked for was to rest and relax without any obligations or bother. Not a care in the world.

She struggled to tune out the noise. Resigned, she struggled to get up. The noise got closer and closer. Bounding, thumping footsteps up the stairs. She sat up, aghast. The bedroom door was thrown open.

"Happy Mother's Day!!!" three excited voices shouted gleefully.

Her eyes blazed widely, lighting up as stars. She smiled, surprised and gleeful. She was no longer tired. At once, she regretted her previous thoughts.

Susie and Andrew plopped onto the bed, each giving her a kiss on her cheek.

Susie waved a card in the air. "Here, Mama! Look!" She gave it to her. It had flowers and butterflies on its cover. She eagerly and joyfully took the card, opened, and read it. She was ecstatic.

"Oh, my darlings!" she exclaimed as she held out her arms for a hug.

"We love you!" the children affirmed joyfully.

"Me, too!" she grinned happily.

Susie held up a box. "Look, Mama, look!" She shoved it in her mother's face eagerly with delight. "Your favorite movies!"

Susie gave it to her. Katherine Josephine took it, fumbling with the wrapping paper and discarding it on the floor without a care. Again, her eyes lit up with gleaming stars.

"Oh, my!" she proclaimed with excitement.

Andrew chimed in, saying, "I know you always loved *Casablanca, The Red Shoes,* and *Gone with the Wind.* You mentioned it several times they were your favorite movies."

Then from behind his back, he showed her his butterfly collection.

"Look, Mom, look what I got you. You do love butterflies, especially blue ones, being you love that color."

"Yes, yes," she reached for it from his hands. "Oh!" She was ecstatic but flabbergasted.

Then, she looked toward Edward Ferdinand, who was carrying a tray.

"Happy Mother's Day, honey," he addressed his wife lovingly. "Pancakes with syrup, two slices of white toast with grape jelly, orange juice, and coffee, just as you like it, dear."

Again, she attempted to speak, but she was so overwhelmed with joy.

"Today is your day," he pointed out to his wife. Then he faced their children. "Right?" he nodded to them. They agreed.

"You do not have to lift a finger. Today is completely your day. Breakfast and lunch in bed while you watch your movies without thinking about anything to worry or care about. We will do whatever needs to be done. Do not worry. Everything is going to be fine."

Again, he faced their children with a smile, "Don't bother your mother for anything. Let her be. Today is her day to enjoy herself and do whatever she pleases, okay?"

The children obediently headed out the door, calling out lovingly to their mother, "We love you!"

Before Edward Ferdinand left their bedroom, he turned toward his wife and gleefully said, "Enjoy your day, honey!"

All three were out the door, which they closed behind them.

Katherine Josephine took out the DVD of *Casablanca*, got out of bed, and inserted it into the DVD player. Then, she took the remote control, got back into bed, and started watching the movie with relish.

She was in heaven. Sheer bliss. Everything copacetic.

9 A.M.

The children sat at the table, chattering away, slurping down their cornflake cereal after they poured the milk in their bowls. Edward Ferdinand sipped his coffee as he read the newspaper. His breakfast consisted of scrambled eggs with three strips of bacon and a glass of orange juice.

"Children," he addressed, "Please, Susie, Andrew, stop making so much noise. Eat like a person ought to. Your mother needs her time alone. You know that."

They paused at once, looking up from their cereal bowls and grudgingly replied,

"Okay, Daddy," Susie acknowledged her father.

Andrew briefly nodded, "Yeah, right."

"All right, children." He resumed reading his newspaper, eating his eggs and picking up a strip of bacon.

Susie and Andrew obediently went back to their breakfast without a sound.

9:45AM

The meal was finished.

"Okay, guys," Edward Ferdinand glanced at the children, "Remember what we said to your mother this morning?"

Both nodded while staring at their father intently, saying nothing.

"We're going to do all the chores Mother always does. Remember?" First, to his daughter, he said, "I want you and Andrew to clear the table, take your dishes to the sink, rinse them, then put them in the dishwasher. I want the appliances and counters spotless, and the floor swept. Afterward, Susie, you dust the living room. And, Andrew, you vacuum."

The children began rising from their chairs, but Edward Ferdinand put his hand up. "I'm not through yet."

They sat back down.

"Andrew, you clean the little bathroom down here. Susie, you do the upstairs bathroom. Okay?" Both nodded again, murmuring under their breaths. "Lastly, I want your rooms cleaned and your beds made. I will be in the garage, sweeping and cleaning. Then, I will be washing the car. You both want your mother to have a good day, don't you?" he inquired of the children.

"Sure," Andrew complied.

Susie, with a cheeky grin, chuckled, "Of course, Daddy."

Edward Ferdinand went on, "You should be finished by 12:30 P.M. I will make you sandwiches for lunch. Susie, you'll have tuna fish salad on toasted rye bread." Then he turned to Andrew, "And you will have peanut butter on white bread, as you prefer. Also, you will have milk and brownies afterward. Now, I am going to repeat what we spoke about before, though I know you will oblige. You are not to bother Mother today for anything. If you need to, please bring it to my attention. Otherwise, you two are to fend for yourselves. Only I can go see her to make sure she is doing fine. You understand, don't you, children?"

However, Susie wailed, "But I want to see how she is doing. And to tell her I love her."

Then, Andrew piped up, "Me, too!"

Edward Ferdinand, without hesitation replied, "I'll tell her what you both said, okay? I promise."

Susie wailed again, "What about Mama's lunch?"

Their father replied gently and kindly, with assurance, "I'll make it and bring it up to her. Don't worry."

They agreed to their father's calm but firm instructions. Then they rose from their chairs and began their chores. Edward Ferdinand put his newspaper down on the table, got up and headed out the door.

2 P.M.

"Children!" Edward Ferdinand called from the top of the stairs.

Susie and Andrew were sitting on the couch. They turned to face him with attentiveness, their eyes wide open.

"I'm immensely proud of all the work you both did in the house. And you did not bother your mother once. Just for that, I am allowing you both to come upstairs to see her. She really wants to see you both, okay, children?"

Susie jumped up and clapped her hands. Andrew automatically said, "Oh, sure!"

They both smiled while bounding up the stairs pushing and almost knocking their father over, who cheerfully cautioned, "Be careful, kids." He was nonplussed and gleamed at them.

They burst into their parents' bedroom. Edward Ferdinand followed as they pounced on the bed.

Katherine Josephine was clad in a long, spaghetti-strap, azure negligee.

"Darlings!" their mother joyfully exclaimed, holding her arms out to them, waiting for their embraces. As they did, she caressed them to her bosom tightly, and kissed their cheeks. They did likewise.

"How are my babies?" she coyishly inquired while they were in her arms.

"Happy Mother's Day, Mama!" Susie cried out gleefully.

Andrew added with a small grin, "I hope you're having a good day. Dad told us not to bother you."

Susie then piped up, "We cleaned the whole house. Just as Daddy asked us to."

"You should see what a good job they did, honey!" Edward Ferdinand exclaimed to his wife.

He went on, "And they didn't gripe or complain once."

"Oh, thank you, thank you all." She was gracious and amicable.

The children hugged and kissed their mother again. Edward Ferdinand pecked her gently on the lips.

The three of them unwound themselves from her and, with bright smiles and shiny sparks in their eyes, announced with gaiety, "You're so very, very welcome."

Then, Edward Ferdinand turned to the children, "And since you made your mother happy on her special day, I'm giving you each twenty dollars to go to the mall to buy whatever you want," he stated as he handed them each a twenty-dollar bill which they accepted graciously, but with great enthusiasm.

"Thank you," said Andrew. Then he asked his father, "Is it all right if I buy this new video game that just came out?"

Then, Susie elatedly chimed in, requesting, "There is a new Lady Gaga DVD movie everyone is raving about. Can I buy it, Daddy?"

Edward Ferdinand grinned at the children.

"Sure, kids," he consented.

They jumped up and down the stairs to the front door. Before they opened it, their father called out, "Be home by 4 P.M., please. We are taking Mother out tonight for Chinese food, her favorite."

"Sure, Dad," Andrew obliged.

They dashed out the door enthusiastically.

Edward Ferdinand watched them. His and Katherine Josephine's children. He was so proud of them. So fortunate to have them. His and Katherine Josephine's children. Their treasures.

5 P.M.

The Clocks were getting ready for their special night out.

Katherine Josephine stood swaying, to and from, in front of her mirror, primping herself up. She was dressed in a long-sleeved floral blue dress. Her red hair was styled with waves around her face. She wore slip-on pumps with small but comfortable heels. She decided to put on her pearl necklace, which went with her pearl earrings. She lovingly faced her husband.

"Do I look all right, dear?"

Edward Ferdinand was adjusting his tie and straightening his white shirt and black pants. Afterward, he put on his blazer. His jet-black, wavy hair was perfectly combed without a strand out of place. He wore black Oxford shoes.

He replied lovingly to his wife, "You're simply beautiful," as he offered to help her with her necklace.

"Here, let me help you with that." He clasped the lock on back of her necklace.

Her eyes sparkled at her husband.

"Here, let me help you with that," she offered while putting her hands under his neck, fixing his tie.

They gazed into each other's eyes with admiration and adoration.

Afterward, Katherine Josephine patted his chest. He kissed her warmly and gently on her lips. She did the same in return.

He put his hands on her shoulders and proudly professed, "You are my queen."

Then, she affirmed with distinction, "And you are my king."

Forever and always.

Then, they heard silly, smirking giggles at their bedroom door. They turned. It was their children.

Susie was wearing a long puffed-sleeved red floral dress that ended above her knees. Over it, she had on a cotton red jacket. She had red plaid sandals on her feet. Her tousled hair hung on her shoulders.

Andrew wore a brown plaid denim shirt with brown dungarees. He had a clip-on tie under his neck. He had a suede light brown jacket over his clothes. His brown leather shoes had buckles on them. His hair was parted perfectly on the side.

Their parents proclaimed their admiration ecstatically.

First their mother, "My darlings!" She was elated.

Then their father pronounced, "You're our prince and princess!" They all laughed at once.

Then, Edward Ferdinand helped his wife get her fur wrap on. He then put on his long black coat. He took his wife's hand. Clasping hand in hand, they headed out. Their children followed behind them.

"Let's go now, everybody!" Edward Ferdinand commanded.

They exited the room and walked down the stairs. Edward Ferdinand held the front door open, first for his wife, then his daughter, and then his son. Afterward, he stepped behind them and they headed to their car. He ushered them in, and they were off.

6 P.M.

The family was seated around the table. Katherine Josephine and Edward Ferdinand chattered away with each other coyishly and flirtatiously, their hands patting each other. The children playfully poked each other's ribs, giggling at some private joke between them. Each family member placed their cloth napkins on their laps, waiting to be served.

Edward Ferdinand ordered tender beef, chicken, shrimp, and roast pork with Chinese vegetables. Katherine Josephine wanted lobster, shrimp, scallop, and crab meat with mixed vegetables and sizzling rice. Susie loved chicken chow mein with white rice, wonton soup, an eggroll, and fried brown pork rice. Andrew opted for crisp boneless duck with mixed vegetables, smeared with brown sauce, topped with almonds.

A tall, thin waiter clad in a white shirt and black pants appeared with their orders.

"Dinner is served," he announced cheerfully to the family. Gently, he handed each of them what they asked for.

The children looked up at him. "Thanks!"

Edward Ferdinand and Katherine Josephine nodded pleasantly at the waiter, who bowed and said with glee, "Enjoy your meal, folks." At that, he left them to their dinner.

After they were served, they started eating with delight, though with gracefulness and proper etiquette—not rushing, gobbling, or wolfing it down. Just enjoying it as they engaged casual, pleasant conversation.

7 P.M.

Everybody's plate was clean.

Edward Ferdinand offered to his family: "Who wants ice cream?"

"Me, me!" The children jumped out of their seats eagerly.

"All right," he confirmed. "First, we'll have tea," he faced his wife, "okay?" She agreed with amity.

Susie had chocolate, Andrew had vanilla, Edward Ferdinand had pistachio, and Katherine Josephine had rocky road.

The family drank their tea and had their desserts with contentment.

8:30 P.M.

They were home. Tired, but happy.

"Time for bed, children," Katherine Josephine quietly told them. "School tomorrow."

"Yes, Mama!" Susie amicably obeyed her mother.

"Yes, Mom," said Andrew, in accordance with his sister's reply.

Susie threw her arms around her mother's neck and kissed her cheek. "I love you. Happy Mother's Day, Mama!"

Andrew briefly hugged her and gave her a peck. "Good night, Mom. And happy Mother's Day, again," he vocalized quietly but sincerely.

"Thank you all for my wonderful day!"

The children dashed up the stairs.

Edward Ferdinand turned to his wife, "Happy, happy Mother's Day, sweetheart," he said, kissing her on the lips. She returned the kiss in kind, with love.

Edward Ferdinand, still gazing at his wife, put his hands on her hips. Slowly, he cupped her face with his hands. Then, she put her hands on the sides of his face and they kissed each other passionately on the lips. They remained in that position for a while, saying nothing. Enjoying the moment.

Leaning over the railing, with smiling faces and twinkling eyes, Susie and Andrew watched their parents.

"To bed now, children," Edward Ferdinand ordered firmly but kindly. Katherine Josephine smiled at them, not saying a word.

It had been another joyful day in the Clock household.

THE CLOCK FAMILY ON VACATION

The cheerful family was all smiles as they rode in the car, gazing at the breathtaking scenery. The sky was a bright blue, the sun was shining, the trees were a fresh green, swaying in the wind, and there were colorful flowers all around. The site was mesmerizing. The family sang off-key, but in joyous, high-pitched voices. Everyone was in love with love, in love with life. No one had uttered a negative thought or displayed a sign of gloom or sullenness.

They were heading toward the beach. Susie and Andrew dashed out of the car, skipped ahead of their parents, plopped down into the hot sand, and began playing. Katherine Josephine and Edward Ferdinand sat down on their lounge chairs, wearing sunglasses and hats. They winked and blew kisses at each other, smiling with gaiety.

A while later, the whole family jumped from their spots and ran into the water, splashing around and laughing to their hearts' content.

EVENING

They ordered their favorite food: Chinese. Everyone dug eagerly into the bowls, ate daintily, though with relish, gusto, and enthusiasm. Simply enjoying their meal and engaging in mundane but pleasant conversation.

That day was the beginning of their idyllic vacation.

They were warm, loving, kind, supporting parents, with playful, obedient, respectful, high-spirited children, all full of life. No harsh words crossed them. Their mother gazed at them with love in her eyes. Their father was quiet and kind. They were all warm and affectionate with each other, enjoying their vacation. No tears were shed among them.

On the way home, everyone was tired but gleeful. It was another wonderful vacation filled with movies, cartoons, a comedian, a magic show, boardwalk strolls, watching the fireworks in the sky, feeding the animals at the zoo, playing catch in the park, pony and boat rides, arcade games, winning big colorful stuffed animals, riding the carousel and the whip and the roller coaster, and touring historical landmarks such as mansions and museums.

Both Susie and Andrew took out their tablets and put on their favorite songs: "Looking Out My Back Door" and "Cotton Fields," both by Creedence Clearwater Revival. They could not get their eyes off the young people, dressed somewhat provocatively, dancing around the floor while smiling and winking at each other, all having a very good time. The children swayed to the cheerful music while leading the band. Andrew could not get his eyes off one of the girls with long, curly, light brown hair, wiggling her behind at the boy behind her. Susie eyed the boy in the white T-shirt, swinging his hips from side to side. Both children giggled gleefully. Their mother turned, facing them with a smile and gleam in her eyes. She loved seeing her children enjoying themselves. It made her very happy, for that was all she wanted for them: to be happy and gay and in love with life. So did their father, who would steal a glance at them in the rearview mirror as he drove his car down the road.

As they entered their home, Susie threw her arms around her mother's neck and kissed her cheek saying, "I love you, Mama." But, Andrew, at age ten, was too embarrassed to display affection like his sister, though he did love his parents. He would still say, with small grin, "I love you, Mom." She understood and was not insulted.

Susie and Edward Ferdinand grabbed each other's hands, and he twirled his daughter around and around, both giggling.

"How's my girl?" he asked.

She laughed and said, "Just peachy, Daddy."

Then Andrew said, "Way to go, Dad!"

They high fived each other as they jumped in the air. Everyone laughed with glee. Then Edward Ferdinand took his wife's hand and kissed her cheek, and she reciprocated with a smile.

Edward Ferdinand and Katherine Josephine turned to their children with a happy grin. "Time for bed, children."

"Good night, Mama, Daddy!" Susie shouted brightly. Andrew followed suit with a shy smile. Both dashed up the stairs, poking each other playfully with their elbows.

Edward Ferdinand then turned to his wife with love. "Honey, it's simply been a long week of fun and joy."

Then he looked at his watch, "but I am tired, and I know you must be, too. So how about we have our own, private fun together in bed, sweetheart?"

Katherine Josephine pecked his cheek. "Certainly, my love."

They grasped each other's hands and made a dash upstairs. They could not wait. This was time for themselves.

The end of their joyous, thrilling vacation. Memories to last forever.

RIGHT TO DIE: A MOTHER'S UNCONDITIONAL LOVE FOR HER FAMILY

Katherine Josephine was sitting in front of her vanity table, clad in a white-lace slip, brushing her long, wavy red hair furiously while looking at herself in the mirror. She smiled and her eyes were glowing.

Edward Ferdinand sat up in bed reading the newspaper. He was deeply engrossed. Suddenly, he laid the paper down on the bed bedside him and asked his wife.

"Are you all right, honey?"

Katherine Josephine turned around toward him and gleefully answered, "Oh, yes, I'm fine," she stated convincingly.

"You've been sitting there for almost an hour," he remarked.

"Oh," she laughed, "I guess I didn't realize it."

"Can't wait until tomorrow. Imagine, honey. We have been married for thirty years. Our children are grown and out of the house busy with their own lives. Our daughter is an assistant editor for a magazine, whose husband is a nice, young man and an Estate Planning and Asset Protection lawyer. Our son is a veterinarian whose wife is a lovely woman who works in a bookstore." Then, he thought, "And we're grandparents. The children are getting so big."

Katherine Josephine kept brushing her hair, not acknowledging her husband. She put the brush down. Then, she gazed into her mirror with a puzzled expression on her face. She said not a word.

"Honey?" he called.

Still looking at her reflection, she still did not respond.

"Honey?" he reiterated with concern.

Abruptly, she faced him not showing any sign of hearing him. She looked at him but did not see him. She heard his voice but was silent.

Edward Ferdinand got out of bed and walked up to her, taking her by her shoulders. She jerked away, a scowl on her face. So, unlike her, he mused.

"Are you all right? I've been talking to you, but you didn't respond."

Suddenly, a big smile crossed her face. She jumped up and threw her arms around her husband. Surprised, but satisfied and relieved. He laughed. She was herself. He was jubilant as he patted her back, and he took her face in his hands and kissed her cheek. She reciprocated and laughed hysterically.

He took her hand, "It's getting late now. Tomorrow is the big day!"

Katherine Josephine sat nonplussed.

"What?" she asked, "tomorrow?"

He looked at her weary-like, "our thirtieth, honey."

She giggled again playfully tapping his chest, "Oh, yes, honey. Oh, yes. Tomorrow. That is right. Our thirtieth wedding anniversary."

He patted her back and they went to bed. Edward Ferdinand turned off the lights.

"Good night, honey," he kissed his wife.

She giggled with a silly grin and said, "I love you."

"Me, too," he replied. He had a very concerned, painful look on his face. *She's not herself. She's acting very strangely.*

He tried dismissing these thoughts. *Probably a change of life, hormonal imbalances. Anyway, she is fifty-four. Women that age do act peculiar. But not Katherine Josephine. She was always so cheerful and bright.* He looked at her, sound asleep. He patted her back and kissed her cheek.

"I love you, darling," he whispered in her ear.

SUNDAY AFTERNOON

Everyone was downstairs preparing for the party. A large red and blue sign hung in the living room. *Happy 30th anniversary, Katherine Josephine and Edward Ferdinand.* Stars and flowers and butterflies surrounded the sign. People were gabbing, sipping their drinks, putting food on their plates.

They were all smiles, laughing with, joking with, and poking each other. They were enjoying themselves and were excited. It was their friends' thirtieth anniversary, God bless them.

But then one guest realized that Katherine Josephine was not yet downstairs.

"Where is Katherine Josephine? I have not seen her all day," he remarked.

Then everyone stopped when he spoke. They gazed around. Katherine Josephine was not there. It was Edward Ferdinand's party and hers—*their* party, for them, the happy couple. It was their day.

Edward Ferdinand turned to his daughter, who now insisted she be addressed by her given name, Susannah Joy, being she was not a little girl anymore, but a grown woman with a career and her own family.

"Susannah Joy," he called. "Would you please go upstairs and see what's with Mama? I'm concerned, and so is everybody here."

She obediently nodded and ascended the stairs.

She opened her parents' bedroom door. She looked around and saw her mother sitting on her bed in her slip, her hair unruly, her face contorted.

"Mama?" she called.

No answer. She sat like a statue.

"What's wrong, Mama? Everyone is waiting for you downstairs. It's yours and Daddy's thirtieth anniversary party."

Katherine Josephine turned and faced her daughter and glared at her, her eyes afire. Still, she uttered not a word.

Susannah was not to be deterred, so she walked up to her and put her arms around her mother's neck, as she had done when she had been a little girl. Katherine Josephine loved that. But now, she pushed her daughter away roughly, anger in her eyes.

Then, with her hand, she smacked Susannah across the face.

Susannah felt the bruised spot.

"Don't touch me!" Katherine Josephine screamed. "Don't you ever touch me, you fuckin' bitch!" She would not stop yelling, tears streaming down her face. Susannah stood in her spot.

"Mama, it's me, your daughter, your darling daughter. You used to call me that when I was a little girl, remember?" She tried to help her mother, who was frightened and confused and helpless. *What is going on?* Susannah pondered to herself. This woman was not her mother. She could not understand her behavior.

"What's going on? What's wrong?" Edward Ferdinand stood by the door.

She looked up at her father, a helpless, distraught expression on her face.

"Daddy," she plaintively started, "there is something wrong with Mama. She is not acting right. When I went to hug and kiss her, as I always do, she yelled at me not to touch her. She called me a bitch. And she smacked me across my face." She started sobbing uncontrollably while touching the spot where she was hit. "Something's wrong, Daddy. She is acting so out of character. It is not normal for her."

Edward Ferdinand sighed and stood.

"It's all right, honey." He stated to his daughter. "Why don't you go downstairs. I'll take care of her."

Susannah nodded and left the room.

Edward Ferdinand walked over to his wife, gently put his hands on the sides of her face, and asked earnestly, "What's the matter, honey? Why did you hit Susannah? She loves you. We all do."

Katherine Josephine mournfully looked up. She was confused. "I'm sorry, I am. I really am. I didn't mean to!" she cried out. "Don't be mad at me."

Still with his hands on her face, he asked, "Why don't you get dressed and fix yourself up? Everyone is waiting for you."

Katherine Josephine lifted her head and smiled. She threw her arms around her husband and kissed him.

He laughed. "Okay, darling."

He left the room. She began getting ready for her and Edward Ferdinand's special event—their thirtieth wedding anniversary. She smiled to herself at the thought. She was joyful. All was well.

"Everything's all right, folks," Edward Ferdinand announced to the guests. "Katherine Josephine was feeling a little under the weather—you know, work, family. She was just tired and stressed out. Women her age tend to get very emotional." He stated this without conviction, wanting to believe his words.

Everyone resumed to their conversation and food.

Minutes later, they heard hysterical, high-pitched laughter. Katherine Josephine was descending the stairs in disarray. Everyone looked up at her with shock, eyes bolting out of their sockets, mouths ajar.

Her red hair was piled on top of her head, disheveled, and her face was smeared with make-up. The spaghetti-straps on her dress hung down her shoulders so that the top of her dress was slipping down, showing her bare breasts. Her slip was hanging, her stockings were running and sagging, and her shoes were wobbly.

Edward Ferdinand shouted with uncontrollable anger at his wife. He did not know what he was saying. He was so overwrought, frustrated, and embarrassed. This was not his wife whom he loved dearly. *What was wrong with her? Why was she behaving like this?*

Everyone stared, too shocked to say anything. They knew not what to say. They had all known Edward Ferdinand and Katherine Josephine for years. They were a loving, wonderful couple. Everyone that knew them loved them because they were friendly, personable, and open-hearted.

Edward Ferdinand dashed up the stairs. "Katherine Josephine!" He shouted her full name. She laughed, completely oblivious to her surroundings.

He took her arm and headed upstairs, then turned to the guests apologetically.

"Excuse us, I'm taking her upstairs. Perhaps she will be all right. This might be a setback, a temporary relapse." He knew not what to say.

He turned toward his wife and lead her into their bedroom and gently sat her down. Katherine Josephine's head was down.

"I'm sorry," she whimpered, "Don't be mad."

He took her face in his hands and gazed into her eyes. "I'm not, but I'm worried."

"Is she all right?" Edward Ferdinand turned and saw his son and daughter near the door.

Suddenly, he said what needed to be said—unfortunate but true: "Your mother is very sick. She needs professional help."

Then he faced his wife. "Lay down and rest, darling. I will be downstairs. We'll talk later." He stroked his wife's shoulder.

Katherine Josephine plopped down on her back on the bed, and remained there.

Edward Ferdinand, with his children, exited the bedroom.

"We all need to talk about your mother."

Susannah and Andrew agreed. Much needed to be said. This could not go on anymore. Edward Ferdinand loved his wife dearly, but she needed more help than he was able to provide her. He watched and waited for her. She was asleep. He closed the bedroom door behind him.

"What will we tell our guests?" Andrew asked, concerned. "They came here to celebrate what was to be a joyous occasion."

Edward Ferdinand patted his shoulder reassuringly. "Don't worry, son. I'll take care of it."

As they descended to the bottom of the staircase, seeing all his and his wife's friends upset and worried, Edward Ferdinand began, "Katherine Josephine is very sick. I knew it, but I refused to acknowledge it. She needs professional help. Her behavior is not her fault. She cannot help it. I am taking her to our family doctor. He will know what to do." Then he paused and resumed, "I am sorry. I know you all came to celebrate what should have been a wonderful occasion to enjoy. And I do not want to be a poor or rude host, but please understand. I regretfully must ask you all to leave. It pains me to say it. I do thank you all for coming, for being our friends, and for your kindness and thoughtfulness. But I do hope you all understand the situation. I will keep you all posted and appreciate your good wishes and love. To be honest, I do not know what is going to happen next. But, again, thank you all for your support. Goodnight."

One guest quipped up, "We do support you, Edward Ferdinand. We do so completely." Then he turned to the other guests. "We do, and we're all very sorry." The others agreed. "We're all worried about Katherine Josephine. She is such a warm, lovely woman." Everyone murmured loudly, in harmony. Then they reached for their coats and bid Edward Ferdinand and his children goodbye and good luck.

"We'll be praying for you. Goodnight."

They left and Edward Ferdinand shut the door.

The family stood in their spot, watching the guests leave. They said not a word, for they did not know what to say or do.

Then, Edward Ferdinand faced them, and began to speak quietly and gently, choosing his words carefully while being calm and composed.

"I'd like everyone to please sit down. We must talk about Katherine Josephine's behavior during the past few days. You all noticed she is not acting as herself. And I am concerned, and I know you are, too, as well."

The hand of an eight-year-old boy shot up. Edward Ferdinand faced him. "Yes, Sean?"

Sean was Andrew's son, whose straight, thin, light brown hair hung down over his mournful brown eyes. He was a serious, sensitive young boy. Edward Ferdinand saw tears in his eyes.

"I noticed stuff, too, Grandpa. You see, the other day, when you and Grandma came to visit us, I saw her standing facing the wall, calling out expletives in a shrieky tone. And when she turned and saw me, she yelled, 'Get the fuck away from me!' Her eyes were afire. I tried to find out what was wrong. She was so upset. Her face turned beet red, and she pushed all the objects off the dresser. I did not tell anyone. I was afraid."

Then a five-year-old girl, his granddaughter, who had shoulder-length, wavy, mousy brown hair and doe-like dark eyes, looked up at him with a sorrowful expression on her face.

"Another time, at our house, Grandma was in the kitchen furiously opening and closing drawers, throwing the silverware around, raging on about someone stealing her purse. I asked her what was wrong. I was trying to help her, Grandpa, honest," she started to cry at the memory, "but she screamed at me and called me a 'fuckin' bitch!' I was frightened. She tried to grab my throat. I was screaming in horror and ran away. Like Sean, I did not tell anyone. I was too scared, Grandpa."

Edward Ferdinand then remarked with reassurance, "It's all right, honey. You did nothing wrong." He paused, then resumed, "Grandma didn't mean it, Donna. She loves you."

Then he turned to the rest of the family. "Your Grandma loves all of you very much. But she is very sick. To be frank, I noticed odd behaviors myself, even before our party. She had put toothbrushes in the refrigerator and books in the oven. She would forget what day it was. She did not even remember having a job."

The rest of the family listened intensively, for they had noticed Katherine Josephine's strange, erratic behaviors, but, as with Edward Ferdinand, had dismissed and explained them away. Katherine Josephine would go into dazes, stand in the middle of the room, misplace important papers, not pay bills, neglect her hygiene, and forget to tend to her basic needs.

Edward Ferdinand glanced around and added, "She's been negligent in taking care of the household. The laundry has piled up, and there are dirty dishes, silverware, pots, and pans laying in the sink, among other things."

Everyone agreed. Katherine Josephine needed serious help. They loved her. But they needed outside professional help.

"I don't think she should go to work tomorrow in her condition. For now, anyway. I'll speak to her supervisor in the morning and explain the situation."

Then he looked at his watch. "I know it is late, but there is a 24/7 housekeeping service agency available downtown. I will give them a call. Hopefully, they can send someone tomorrow. I will tell them it is imperative and explain the circumstances. Okay, everyone?"

They all agreed.

Paige, Andrew's wife, who wore her black hair in a bob under her ears and had dark, pleasant eyes, pointed her finger upward. "I can always check on her when I am not at work." She worked part-time as an assistant in a local bookstore.

Edward Ferdinand thanked her, "That's very kind of you, Paige."

Susannah then spoke, "I'll come after work, but I'll have to bring Ariana. She should at least see her grandmother and get to know her." Ariana was four years old. She had ash-blonde, wavy hair and hazel eyes. She was always smiling and leaping about. She was a bundle of energy.

Susannah looked down at her daughter, who was sitting on her lap. "All right, sweetheart?"

Ariana made a huge grin at her mother. "Grandma!" she spoke proudly.

Susannah bounced her up and down and gleefully complimented her: "That's right!"

Then Edward Ferdinand continued, clasping his hands together in front of his chest, "I think that about covers everything." Seeing his grandchildren yawning and nodding off, he stated, "The children are very tired. It was a very exhausting day for them. It's bedtime now, everybody."

At that, the whole family rose from their seats, gathered their coats and bags, and led the children out. They all said goodbye to each other. They went out the door. Edward Ferdinand shut it behind them.

He then went to call the agency. He began dialing. "Hello, my name is Edward Ferdinand Clock," he said into the telephone.

MORNING

Edward Ferdinand laid in bed and glanced at his wife. She was sound asleep. He wanted to touch her gently, to show her he loved her dearly, but then thought, *let her sleep. She needs quiet.*

He got out of bed, took off his pajamas, and put on his robe and slippers. Gently, he opened the bedroom door, left, closed it again, quietly, and tiptoed downstairs with care.

The doorbell rang. He went to answer it. It was Mrs. Mackenzie from the agency. *Right on time.* He offered her a chair at the table, and she sat down. They shook hands.

She had a roly-poly figure, a short stature, and a full face. Her straight, dark hair was pulled back in a bun. Her dark eyes were deadpan, but she had a pleasant smile on her lips.

"Glad you're early," he stated. "I'd like for you to get acquainted with your duties—especially caring for my wife. She needs complete care. We do not know exactly what her problem is but, as I said on the telephone, she has not been acting like herself—not loving, kind, happy, or cheerful. She is disorientated, confused, forgetful, negligent, hostile, and violent. She cannot take care of herself as she used to. She always did what had to be done, and everyone admired how patient, kind, and thoughtful she was to her family and friends. We were always a loving, harmonious family, and got along splendidly. Now, she acts out and yells for no apparent reason. Last night, when our daughter tried to comfort her with a hug and a kiss, she hit her across the face and called her a 'fuckin' bitch.' She never, ever has done that. Not ever. She loves our daughter very much. And our family members have also witnessed her erratic behaviors—especially my son's children. They were very frightened. For a while, I, myself noticed her sloppy hygiene and negligent and careless housekeeping. But I kept dismissing these behaviors and would explain them away as a change of life or stress from work or from planning our thirtieth wedding anniversary, which was yesterday. It was a disaster. She came downstairs completely disheveled, unkempt, and half naked. I really do not want to elaborate. I will call our family doctor in a few minutes to make an appointment. And we will take it from there. I hope you understand the situation. And I will not blame you if you feel this is too much for you, Mrs. Mackenzie."

She tapped her fingers on the tabletop. "I get everything you said, Mr. Clock. I have been in this line of work for fifteen years and there was never a time I refused any job, whatever it was. Yours does seem a bit challenging, but I'm willing, sir."

Edward Ferdinand smiled. "That's great." Then he continued, "I'll go bring her down now, okay? So, you can get acquainted."

She nodded and he ascended the stairs.

"Come on." He gently nudged Katherine Josephine. "It's time to get up, honey." She just lay there. Suddenly, she opened her eyes and faced him, with a puzzled, blank look on her face. She just stared.

He patted her arm. "Let us go downstairs, sweetheart. We will have breakfast. There is someone waiting to meet you. She is going to help. Okay, darling?"

Katherine Josephine just stared through her husband, saying nothing.

He gently took her hand. Finally, she let him.

"I'll help you get dressed, all right?" he asked her. She still said nothing but obeyed without protest.

"That's my girl." He patted her back and winked.

He gave her underwear and a housecoat to put on after she took off her clothes from yesterday. He took a barrette and put her hair in a low ponytail. He washed her face and hands and, with some difficulty, got her teeth brushed. He directed her to her mirror and cried out, "How beautiful you are, my darling!" He was excited. Then he fetched her slippers and slid them on her feet. He then led her by her hand, slowly, down the steps.

Mrs. Mackenzie stood up and watched. *What a wonderful, loving, caring husband*, she thought to herself.

He led her to a chair at the kitchen table. He sat her down, took her face in his hands, and kissed her cheek. She jerked away.

He pointed to Mrs. Mackenzie and introduced her, "Honey, this is Mrs. Mackenzie. She is going to be with you, all day, to help you. She'll keep you company."

Katherine Josephine shouted out, "I have to go to work!!" She began to get up, but he gently sat her down.

"Not today, sweetheart. You need help. You are in no condition to go to work." He tried to explain it to her, but to no avail.

Katherine Josephine screamed and jumped out of her chair. "No! I want to go to work!!" She stamped her feet furiously and knocked her chair over. Then she pushed her husband away. He almost fell backward.

Mrs. Mackenzie chimed in, "Sir, let me try, all right? Meanwhile, you go upstairs and do what you must. I will take care of her. I've done this before."

"Thank you, Mrs. Mackenzie." He headed up the stairs.

Katherine Josephine continued her tantrum, slamming and throwing objects around the room, screaming with rage.

"Mrs. Clock," Mrs. Mackenzie gently began as she extended her hand and stroked Katherine Josephine's back. "It's all right. Let us have some breakfast and we'll talk, okay?"

Katherine Josephine jerked away, still in an angry fit, but Mrs. Mackenzie refused to be deterred. She put her hands on her shoulders. "Look at me," she calmly instructed. "Everything will be okay. I am your friend. I am going to help you. We'll have a nice chat."

Her tantrum slowly died down. She stood there in a daze and uttered not a word.

Mrs. Mackenzie gently stroked her hand and led her, without a tussle, toward the table. Katherine Josephine obliged quietly, without a word.

When Katherine Josephine was seated, Mrs. Mackenzie smiled at her, stroking the back of her head.

"Now, how about some breakfast?" she asked her rhetorically. "Your husband says you like scrambled eggs."

Katherine Josephine looked at her in silence. Mrs. Mackenzie went into the kitchen and began preparing the meal.

As he prepared to go to work, Edward Ferdinand called his wife's supervisor, "Hello, Mrs. Adamson." He paused, then continued, "It's

Edward Ferdinand, Katherine Josephine's husband. About my wife, she . . ." he paused.

Then Mrs. Adamson spoke, "Mr. Clock, your wife no longer works here. She hasn't for over a month."

Edward Ferdinand dumbfoundedly asked, "What do you mean, Mrs. Adamson? She left for work every single day!"

Mrs. Adamson went on, "I know she did. She came to the shop a few times, angry and disheveled, thinking she still worked here. I told her nicely to please leave and explained to her, time and again, that she no longer worked for me. But she'd create a scene and I'd have to call security to escort her out."

Edward Ferdinand was still confused. "Why was she let go? You said she was one of your best salesladies. All the customers and staff loved her!"

"She was, Mr. Clock, but I suddenly noticed erratic, inappropriate behaviors. She came in late. Her appearance was always in disarray. And she would snap at the customers, get the orders mixed up, misplace important papers, and hide money in the cabinets. I tried to help her. I did not want to fire her, but I had to. I had no choice. We were losing customers. I explained that her actions were inappropriate, but she shouted expletives at me. Everyone in the shop stared in aghast. They were stunned and speechless. It was so unlike her, Mr. Clock. I am afraid to say it, but your wife does need professional help. I am sorry, Mr. Clock." Mrs. Adamson glanced toward the entrance. "Mr. Clock, I must go now. I have customers waiting to be served. Again, I am truly sorry to have to have told you all this. Have a good day." She hung up the telephone.

Edward Ferdinand stared at the receiver. He could not believe it. *Katherine Josephine got fired and kept it from me all this time. Didn't she figure that I would notice no weekly paycheck coming in?* But he came to understand everything. *What was the use?* he reasoned. *She has been sick all this time and her employer now tells me.*

However, it did no good for him to confront his wife. *She does not and cannot help herself anymore*, he pondered sadly. He decided to say nothing to her. It was not her fault. None of it was.

Then the telephone rang. He picked it up.

"Daddy?" It was Susannah.

"Hi, honey," he addressed her. His voice was tense and quivering.

"Daddy, what's wrong? What happened? Is it about Mama?" She knew it was.

He began with Mrs. Adamson's report that she had had to let her mother go. "She was not acting right, and Mrs. Adamson said she was losing customers because of it."

Susannah listened and said nothing. She did not know what to say. Then, she asked about Mrs. Mackenzie.

"She seems very competent and willing, though she did mention that Mama was a challenge. But that did not dissuade her. When I brought Mama down to meet her, she flew into a fit. She would not let me kiss or hug her. So, Mrs. Mackenzie asked me to let her handle Mama. And I went upstairs. Mama seems fine for now. Mrs. Mackenzie has such patience, and an understanding attitude. She has done this work for fifteen years, and nothing deters her. I think that's good." Edward Ferdinand glanced at his watch. "Honey, I'm going to call Dr. Parone now, to set up an appointment for Mama. Then, I must be getting to the office," he stated.

"I understand completely, Daddy," she affirmed. "I've got to get Ariana ready for school and myself to work. There is a presentation scheduled for this morning and I must be there to help set it up. Bye, Daddy, have a good day! Love you!"

"Love you, too, honey." The call ended.

He started punching in the doctor's telephone number.

"Good morning. Dr. Parone's office," the receptionist greeted brightly. "How may I help you?"

"Denise," he addressed her. "It's Edward Ferdinand Clock. May I please speak with the doctor? It is about my wife. It's imperative that I talk to him."

"Sure, Mr. Clock. I'll go see if he is available, all right?"

Edward Ferdinand held the receiver anxiously. Katherine Josephine needed help badly; she was getting more and more irrational. He knew it was not her fault. He did not blame her. He loved her dearly and always would. Still, he was on pins and needles.

"Mr. Clock," Denise said into the telephone, "he's on an important long-distance call. I did explain your dire situation to him, and he said the minute he is through on the telephone, he will return your call. He promised. So, just be patient and hold tight, all right?"

"Sure, Denise, thank you." He hung up.

He sat on the edge of his bed, wiggling his fingers together—a habit of his when he was tense and nervous. His eyes never left the phone. *Come on, come on*, he pleaded inside himself, willing the phone to ring.

R-r-ring!

He leaped off the bed and dashed to pick up the telephone. He was breathless with anticipation.

"Mr. Clock, it's Dr. Parone. What is the problem? Denise informed me it was urgent," Dr. Parone said with deep concern.

"It's my wife, Doctor. She is not acting right. Her behavior has become so unglued. I cannot help her. The whole family has noticed. You see, Doctor, at first, I did not really pay attention, and pooh-poohed certain behaviors. I tried asking myself, *am I imagining it? Is it real?* This is not like her. At first, I thought it was menopause, as she is fifty-four years old, a common age for a woman to go through it. Or I thought it might be a chemical or hormonal imbalance. That does occur in women. But not my wife, who has always been sweet and loving and a joy to be around. Everyone loves her. But her employer had to fire her. I found out this morning. She said her conduct frightened her and she could not understand it, since Katherine Josephine was her best saleslady. She had no choice but to let her go. She also said she needed extremely intensive care. All these people cannot be wrong. I kept dismissing and overlooking this stuff, and thought it was just a phase, a setback: that it would pass. She will not even let me touch or kiss her. She has gotten violent with our daughter, whom she loves dearly. I know she does. They always had such a tight bond between them. She neglects herself, the household, *everything*, Doctor. I need help. We all do; her as well as the rest of the family. I don't know what else to do."

Dr. Parone had been listening attentively, absorbing everything Edward Ferdinand explained to him.

"I do understand, Mr. Clock." He turned toward Denise and asked for his datebook. He resumed, "Let me see what I can do. From what you have told me, your situation is very frightening and serious— more than you are able to fathom or deal with—so you have overlooked a lot. But you are right, Mr. Clock." As he flipped through his datebook, he stopped on a page and continued, "Luckily, I have an opening tonight at 6 P.M. Bring her in. You are lucky. I had a cancellation. Okay, sir?"

"Oh, thank you very much, Doctor." He showed his profuse appreciation. "I'll bring her in tonight, Doctor. Thanks again."

He hung up the telephone and sighed heavily afterward. Then he checked his watch. Under his breath, he stated nonchalantly, "I'll be a little late. But it is all right. I own the business. I'll have Martin open up."

He then reached for his cellphone and punched in Martin's number. Martin answered. Edward Ferdinand informed him that he will be a little late due to personal reasons. He did not have to know about his beloved wife's deteriorating mental condition. It was not of his concern. However, Martin obliged his request to open up the office.

Then Edward Ferdinand removed his nightclothes and reached for a beige suit and white shirt. Afterward, he checked himself in the mirror, patting his chest. He was pleased. He grabbed his wallet, keys, and cellphone, and headed downstairs. He saw Mrs. Mackenzie and Katherine Josephine at the kitchen table. Mrs. Mackenzie had made herself a cup of tea. Katherine Josephine was eating her breakfast of scrambled eggs and toast. She was quiet.

Edward Ferdinand walked over and asked Mrs. Mackenzie, "Is she all right?"

She smiled agreeably as she watched his wife, who was deeply absorbed in her meal.

Edward Ferdinand began: "Honey." He put his hand on her shoulder. At first, she jumped up, and faced her husband, saying nothing.

"I love you," he stated, and then kissed her cheek. She did not reciprocate the gesture. But he resumed, "Sweetheart," he put his hand on her shoulder, "I have to go to the office now. I am late, but it is all right. You're worth it." Then he kissed the top of her head. She did not flinch. "Goodbye, my darling."

She went back to her food.

He nodded at Mrs. Mackenzie, and she said, "Don't worry, sir. I'm handling it." Then she turned toward Katherine Josephine and said, "We will have a good time together today, won't we? Just you and me, okay?"

Katherine Josephine did not acknowledge her or her husband. But neither were deterred. Mrs. Mackenzie was sure and confident. And Edward Ferdinand loved his wife with all his heart and always would, no matter what. However, he was very distraught and devastated. Hopefully, the doctor would be able to find out what the problem was and take it from there.

Edward Ferdinand grabbed his coat and left.

Mrs. Mackenzie turned and smiled at Katherine Josephine, still talking to her, knowing she would not respond. But it did not faze her. She insisted on doing her job the way she saw fit. She was known to be a very patient and tolerant person. She needed to be, in her line of work. Katherine Josephine would be an odious ordeal to reckon with, but she was fine with it.

Suddenly, Katherine Josephine jumped out of her chair, throwing her plate, filled with food, across the room, and the glass of orange juice on the floor. She started screaming, in tears, "Where is he?!" She was hysterical.

Mrs. Mackenzie got up and tried to comfort her by taking her hand gently into hers, but she snatched it away.

"He left me!" she cried bitterly.

Mrs. Mackenzie patted Katherine Josephine's hand, "Who?"

"Him, that man," she pointed to a photograph of Edward Ferdinand and her embracing and smiling at each other lovingly.

"He went to work, like he does every day," Mrs. Mackenzie stated softly, again taking her hand tenderly.

"Come, Katherine Josephine, let's sit down." She showed her to a chair.

Katherine Josephine stamped her foot hard on the floor.

"Don't call me that!" she demanded angrily.

Gently, Mrs. Mackenzie said, "That's your name. It's so pretty."

Katherine Josephine refused to acknowledge her.

"Don't say that! Ever!"

"What do you want me to call you? Tell me and I'll do it." She truly meant it, trying to placate her.

Arrogantly, her back straight, her head high, her shoulders back, smiling a sweet, small smile, her eyes shining as stars, she answered, "Call me Katie Jo." She had not been called that since she had been a little girl. But she was behaving like one. Mrs. Mackenzie reasoned to herself: *Well, if that is what she wants, what the heck?*

"All right," she began, "Katie Jo."

She jumped up gleefully, laughing like a hyena, and danced around the room. She grinned joyfully. She was happy. Mrs. Mackenzie was satisfied. *At least she is in a good tranquil mood. Well, what can I say? If that is what she prefers to be called, it is fine with me.* There was nothing wrong with being joyful and elated.

"I'm sorry I ruined our breakfast," she apologized. "I'll help you clean it up. It was me who made the mess."

"It's all right . . . Katie Jo." She almost forgot. "It's no problem. You go sit down in the living room. I'll be there in a minute."

She nodded with satisfaction and obediently went to sit down on the couch in the living room, which was surrounded by family photographs. She gazed at them with interest and sighed pleasantly.

She called out: "Miss . . . uh . . . uh," she tried to think of her name, so Mrs. Mackenzie stated it in support: "Mrs. Mackenzie, Katie Jo."

"Uh, yeah, Mrs. . . . Mrs. Mackenzie."

"That's right!"

"My daughter is a writer. She works as an assistant editor for a magazine," with a finger on her lips, she said, "but for the life of me, I cannot think of its name."

"That is all right, Katie Jo. Sometimes I cannot remember certain things myself, either. Don't worry."

"She works hard at her job. She's up for a promotion or raise or something." She became silent. "I'm so proud of my baby girl. I love her with all my heart." She hugged herself. She was beaming with delight.

Mrs. Mackenzie smiled. Katie Jo was jubilant. And to think that this morning she had been so sullen and angry, refusing to communicate or acknowledge anyone. But now she was sharing herself, opening up.

"My son is a . . . a . . . a-animal d . . . doctor," she struggled to find the right word. She became frustrated, and was at a loss.

Mrs. Mackenzie softly reassured her, "It's all right. A lot of people cannot remember every little detail."

Katie Jo smiled and clapped her hands. She gazed at the photographs of her children with a gleam in her eyes.

"They are the apples of my eyes. My precious, darling, joyful angels."

Mrs. Mackenzie was smiling. "How lovely, Katie Jo." She went back to the kitchen and began cleaning up. She was fine. For now, anyway.

"Also, Miss, Miss . . . M . . . Mack . . .." She could not think of the rest of her name.

She took a photograph of Edward Ferdinand off the top shelf and ran up to Mrs. Mackenzie, pushing it into her face while she was drying a dish, "Look, look."

Mrs. Mackenzie faced her.

"This is Edward Ferdinand, my husband, my beloved. He is so wonderful. And so smart. And successful. He runs a . . . a . . . a . . . b . . . business. He owns a . . . a . . . a . . . CPA firm. He used to be a b . . . b . . . book . . . k . . . keeper. A long time ago. He works so hard, Miss. And he loves me. He does." She danced and leaped around the room, laughing the way a little girl would.

Mrs. Mackenzie smiled, "I know he does, dear. I mean, Katie Jo. I can see that."

She watched her. She was so hyper, so excited, and cheerful as a child. But at least she was not violent or out of control, for the moment.

6 P.M.

Katie Jo heard the key turn into the lock at the front door.

"It's him!" she exclaimed delightedly as she bounced off the couch. She smiled in elation.

She pounced up and threw the photo album that she had been looking at for a while down on the sofa.

She had insisted that her hair and face be made up, as she wanted to look beautiful for her husband. Mrs. Mackenzie accommodated her requests. She mused, *at least she is in a happy mood, and not yelling or raging or acting out.* It was her job to be there to help her, and she did so.

Katie Jo had her hair piled up and tendrils at the sides of her face, which was made up impeccably. She was and felt beautiful, just as Edward Ferdinand always thought of her.

She ran up to the door. Edward Ferdinand entered, and she threw her arms around his neck, giving him a peck on his lips. He was very surprised, since she had rebuffed him this morning. Yet, he was jubilant, and laughed nervously.

Then he pulled her back and noticed her face and hair. "You look simply ravishing, my darling," he stated enthusiastically.

Then, with excitement, she told him, "I wanted to look nice for you."

"You will always be beautiful to me," he said sincerely, with a twinkle in his eyes and a smile. They both laughed.

"My darling," he said, reciprocating her affection.

"I love you," she stated anxiously, her arms still around him.

"I love you, too, my darling." They stayed in that position for a few seconds.

Mrs. Mackenzie was drying a plate while watching them. She was so pleased Katie Jo was in this mood. For the present moment, anyway.

"Mr. Clock," she began, "I left some dinner for you—Salisbury steaks with peas and carrots. I hope you do not mind, but Katherine Josephine—no, I mean Katie Jo—was very hungry. She planned on waiting to eat with you and is sorry she did not. You're not upset, are you, sir?"

He smiled. "Not in the least." Then he asked, "Why did you call my wife Katie Jo? She hasn't been called that in a thousand years."

"Sir," she began, "she asked me to. It made her happy, and that is all we want, right? Just for now."

"All right," he agreed, with great hesitation, "just for now. There's no harm in it."

He faced his wife. "Honey, please get dressed now. After I eat dinner, we are going to Dr. Parone for a check-up, okay?

She leaped up and down, then faced Edward Ferdinand, saying nothing—just standing and staring.

Gently, he moved her arms down to her sides.

"Do you love me?" she asked plaintively.

He took her face into his hands and kissed her on the lips. "Always and forever."

Silently, she turned and headed up the steps. He watched her. Mrs. Mackenzie went back to the kitchen to heat up Edward Ferdinand's meal.

It was 7:30PM. Edward Ferdinand and Katherine Josephine were seated in Dr. Parone's office.

"My wife's behavior during these past few months has not been normal. She has been out of control, and that is not like her at all. She has always been kind, loving, and friendly. But now, everything is drastically different, and it is not good. In fact, her behavior does not seem to be improving, though there have been moments of lucidity and love and joy. And it is at those times I felt I was wrong. But not anymore. The whole family has noticed these strange and erratic behaviors." Then he paused and said, "Also, though I never confronted her about her being let go from her job, I knew something was not right. Her employer mentioned it to me. At first, I did not understand, because my wife was the best saleslady she ever had. However, recently, she saw disturbing behaviors in her, and business got bad. She was sorry she had to let her go, but she did not have a choice. She even told me that Katherine Josephine—no, Katie Jo, as she insists I now call her—is in dire need of a specialist doctor." He looked at his wife, who had said not a word, but was glaring at him, her back up, stiffly.

He started trying to remember everything that needed to be mentioned, including how their thirtieth wedding anniversary party, which was supposed to have been a celebration for them, was a total disaster, and how everyone was very concerned about her, since she had always been a lovely, wonderful, warm human being whom everyone enjoyed being with. Edward Ferdinand was tired, sad, and weary, though he continued to speak. There was no going back. Dr. Parone listened to his every word, jotting down notes on his notepad.

Katie Jo stared at her husband with anger in her eyes, her fists clenched. She shrieked at him, "Why are you making fun of me like I am a nutcase or a screwball? Talking about me like I'm invisible!"

He patted her hand and gently stated, "We're all trying to help you. Your conduct has not been appropriate lately. You yell, you forget things, you get confused, you hit our daughter, you will not let anyone touch you or show you love, you don't take care of yourself properly, you neglect your responsibilities."

She paid him no heed and shouted, "I make mistakes! Everyone does! You're making such a big deal—as though I killed someone!!"

He continued, while holding her hand, "Honey," he looked into her eyes mournfully, "all our friends and family told me practically the same type of incidents. They cannot be all wrong. The mistakes you make cause a lot of upset and concern. They are not just ordinary—plainly forgetting or misplacing stuff."

She yelled out, "I said it many times—and how many times do I have to say it?!—*I'm sorry*. I didn't mean it!"

"We know, darling, but you do so more and more lately. And it does not seem to ebb by itself. You might cause deep harm. I know you do not mean or intend to do what you do, but you cannot help it. And the doctor must know everything, so he can help you. That is why we are here. For you. We want you to get better."

Katie Jo fell silent, her head down. She mumbled dejectedly, "All right, whatever."

Then Edward Ferdinand faced the doctor, who said, "I would like your wife to have some X-rays done, such as a C-scan, MRI, and PET scan. There is a room for them down the hallway. The tests will not take long—perhaps a half hour. And afterward, I will administer some tests, in which I will ask her questions. I will go over the results with you. But while I am questioning her, I would like her to be alone, because I feel your presence may unintentionally cause her to get distracted, or you might get impatient and be tempted to 'help' her. You do understand, don't you, sir?"

Edward Ferdinand agreed. "Of course."

Dr. Parone told Denise to show Mrs. Clock to the examination room and to lead her husband out into the waiting room. He began preparing the tests in the meantime. Katie Jo eyed him with suspicion. She was agitated, pouting—her face contorted, her body tense. After a few minutes, she let Denise escort her out the door.

TWO HOURS LATER

Dr. Parone wiggled his fingers on the top of his desk. He had to tell them the results of what he found from the X-rays and oral tests he gave her, and it was not good at all. He would need to tell them what arrangements had to be made, and it was going to be heart-wrenching for them and everyone they knew. Unfortunately, there was no cure or treatment currently available. All they could do was to make Katie Jo comfortable, and to love and appreciate her as they always had. He was not going to sugarcoat or offer false hope about the situation. It was not going to be an easy journey, things would not improve, and she would eventually deteriorate into a helpless human being, totally incapacitated and dependent on her environment, not knowing if she was living or dead. Life was not fair, he knew that. But this was cruelty. It was not a fair deal for them. No one deserved this kind of treatment in life. Katie Jo and her family were good, kind-hearted people, who everyone loved and respected. But this was the beginning of the end. All he could do was give them his sympathy and comfort them. Perhaps grief counselling could be set up for the family. But right now, he had to do the most odious task: informing them of the deeply dismal, hopeless results of the tests.

With both his hands under his chin, he began solemnly, "Mr. and Mrs. Clock . . . ."

As they listened to his heart-wrenching and bleak diagnoses, Katie Jo shut her eyes tightly. Trying to control her tears, she shuddered. Edward Ferdinand watched her, put his arm around her, and held her to his chest, patting her back. They stayed that way for a bit. Dr. Parone watched them with helplessness in his eyes. He tried to offer them solace, handing them packets of information about Katie Jo's condition. Alzheimer's disease and other dementia forms.

Edward Ferdinand took them and quietly stated to Dr. Parone: "We'll handle it." Then, he helped his wife up and, with his arm around her, began to leave. He turned toward the doctor. "We'll be in touch, Doctor, if anything happens."

"Good luck," Dr. Parone offered. He knew not what else to say as he watched them head out the door. *Such a cruel fate.*

As they rode home, Edward Ferdinand faced his wife at times and squeezed her hand. She turned to face him but said nothing for a while. Then she blurted out, "I love you, Edward Ferdinand." He said it back, "Forever and ever." They spent the rest of the ride home in silence.

When they arrived home, Edward Ferdinand got out of the car to let his wife out. She sat like a statue, staring ahead blankly. He opened the door and held out his hand. "Let us go, honey. We're home now," he stated.

Slowly, she turned and faced him. He took her hand and let her in the house.

Mrs. Mackenzie was stood by the door and asked, "Is everything all right, sir, ma'am?"

Edward Ferdinand did not wish to get into it with her at that moment, but he stated, "We'll talk tomorrow. You could go now, Mrs. Mackenzie. We'll see you in the morning."

"Goodnight," she said as she reached for her coat and handbag.

Edward Ferdinand led his wife to a chair in the kitchen. When both were seated, Katherine Josephine began, "I know what I want to do, Edward Ferdinand, and I think I should tell you now while I'm still lucid. But do write down what I say if I forget it." She pushed a pad and pencil to him. He was ready.

"I know what I want to do," she began hesitantly but firmly. "I never thought it would come to this, so I never considered even mentioning it, because I always assumed you'd go first. But, as you know, that is not going to happen. I have long thought that if I were to become afflicted with an incurable or untreatable disease or illness, I would not want you and our children and grandchildren to suffer and be burdened. It is not fair to you or them. We both know that, as the doctor informed us, my disease will progress. I will be totally dependent on my environment, and a burden to you. I want you to remember me as I was, not as how I will eventually end up—as a vegetable, knowing no one, including you and our loved ones. You all should be able to live your own lives as you choose to see fit, and not be responsible for a family member who will never recover and live a full life. I want you all to be happy. I love you all. Thus, I want to die with by voluntary euthanasia, which is assisted suicide with an injection of a barbiturate. I want to go peacefully, in my own bed. I want to do this because I am afraid that I might, in one of my raging episodes, unintentionally cause harm to a loved one, and I want to prevent that from happening."

Edward Ferdinand took in every word she spoke with great clarity. Even though she had this devastating, cruel disease that would rob her of her dignity, she was still a lovely, caring wife and mother.

However, he did say, "Honey, you'll never be a burden to us. Our job is to take care of our loved ones when they are sick. We would love to take care of you. We all love you. You always took great care of all of us, through thick and thin."

Katherine Josephine gazed at her folded hands on the table, then looked at her husband. "I know you feel that way. But, as I already said, it would not be fair for all of you to give up your lives for a family member who will one day be completely incapacitated, unaware, and dependent. I do not want any of you to see me as a vegetable. You all need to live and do things and have fun times with the family and your friends. I know I am only fifty-four, and that is young. But that is the way it is, I'm sorry to say."

He jumped up from across the table, grabbed the sides of her face, and kissed her on both her cheeks. "Oh, honey, you're the most selfless human being on the planet. I love you so!"

Both laughed.

"We'll tell Mrs. Mackenzie tomorrow morning. Then, after work, we will invite the children over and tell them after supper." Edward Ferdinand stated, "And, thank God, we have a son-in-law who happens to be an estate planner and asset protection lawyer, who will be able to help us. We will explain the situation and draw up the appropriate documents. He and I will talk to Dr. Parone. He said he would help us. Okay, honey?" he smiled at his wife, and she did so at him.

"I'm tired now, Edward Ferdinand. Let us go to bed now," she said abruptly and quietly.

They got out of their chairs, and he led her upstairs.

THE FORMALITIES-A WEEK LATER

Each family member sat at an extended rectangular table in Judge Hamilton's chamber. They waited with great anticipation for his arrival. They were all tense and could not decide if this occasion, unusual as it was, could be defined as happy or sad. A beloved family member had been diagnosed with Alzheimer's disease, which was both untreatable and incurable. It would slowly take over her whole self, and leave her completely dependent and incapacitated, a vegetable without the ability to function on her own. She refused to have her loved ones sacrifice their lives for her. She wanted them to remember her as she was—a warm, kind human being, loved by everyone who had the pleasure of knowing her—and not for what she would end up being like—deteriorating and disintegrating into a shell of a person. She hated the thought of it. Her family thought about it and discussed it among themselves. It was sad that she had this cruel illness of memory loss, leaving her a mental cripple, depriving her of a wonderful, joyful life with her family. But they were glad she could die knowing she was loved for her selflessness toward others.

Judge Hamilton entered the room. Everyone stood at their seats, awaiting his arrival to begin the proceedings. When he was ready, everyone sat down.

He put on his specs and started reading the document at hand.

"From what I am seeing, this form is a right to die document requested by Katherine Josephine Parke Clock, a victim of Alzheimer's disease." He gazed at her, and she leaned forward. "That's correct, your Honor."

The judge resumed, "And your family understands and honors your wishes to terminate your life through euthanasia—in another words, assisted suicide by an injection of a barbiturate. You say you want to die peacefully at home in your own bed, correct, Mrs. Clock?"

Katherine Josephine nodded firmly, though slowly.

He continued, "you say you don't want to burden your family and have them see you descend into a completely helpless state of existence—in another words, turn into an infant-like person. You want them to live their lives fully and happily, and to remember and love you as you were?" He took off his specs and remarked, "You are definitely a very self-sacrificing, altruistic, caring individual. I can see why your family loves you. And that you love them that much."

She nodded again, with a slight smile. Edward Ferdinand lovingly took her hand in his.

The judge laid the document down. A clerk came up to him and handed him another form, which he read aloud. He faced a man on his right and started, "It says here that you, Dr. Cornell, will administer the drug, and have two technicians set up the machine in Mrs. Clock's bedroom." Dr. Cornell nodded in agreement. The judge went on, "The date of this special happy-sad family event will take place this Friday, at 8 P.M. Dr. Cornell will arrive early to prepare. Everyone will be downstairs saying their goodbyes to Mrs. Clock. Then, she will be escorted upstairs to her room. And it will be done."

He faced her family and said, "You'll all be told when it's over."

To Katherine Josephine, he said, "You can decide for yourself what you want to wear, all right?"

Again, she agreed. Luckily, her illness had not progressed that much. Even though this disease was known to be unpredictable, Katherine Josephine was able to be lucid at times since she had been ill for less than four months. Everyone was grateful for that.

Then the judge passed a form around for everyone to sign that made sure they clearly understood that Katherine Josephine's assisted suicide was consensual. They were all tired, but relieved the formalities were over. Everyone rose and left. Everything was all set and in order.

FRIDAY, EARLY EVENING

The whole family waited in the living room. They were there to say their goodbyes to their beloved family member, who loved everyone selflessly and unconditionally. She would be missed, but never forgotten—in their hearts forever. Luckily, she was still lucid to make this drastic, heart-breaking decision out of her love for them. She wanted them to live and enjoy their lives, as they were entitled to do.

It was a sad occasion, true, but an altruistic act. She knew what she wanted to do and was sure and everyone understood that this decision had not been made in haste, but with deep contemplation and care. She had thought it through, and knew it was the right decision. She did not want anyone to see her as a braindead shell of a person, her mind completely gone. It was too heart-wrenching. She always wanted everyone to be happy and enjoy their lives. This was her family, who she loved—and who loved her back, unconditionally, in return.

Mrs. Mackenzie was busy fixing Katherine Josephine up in her bathroom. She was smiling as she brushed her hair and put it up. Katherine Josephine wanted to wear her blue halter dress, with a blue butterfly pin in the middle, between her breasts. She put on rouge and red lipstick. Her eyes were made up in blue eyeshadow and her eyelashes were curled up. Neither said a word for a while.

Suddenly, Katherine Josephine blurted out with great excitement: "You've been so great with the children!"

Mrs. Mackenzie just stood and stared. Katherine Josephine was having a delusion, but she just listened. She knew not to correct someone in her condition, but instead smiled. "It's been a pleasure caring for them. They're simply great kids."

"Susie is my darling, you know, don't you?" she asked.

Mrs. Mackenzie nodded and smiled, "She is, Katherine Josephine."

"And Andrew. He's good," Katherine Josephine stated flatly.

"Would you like to see them now? They're all waiting downstairs." She went on.

Mrs. Mackenzie then stated, "Not now. I am sorry. Maybe another time, all right?" Katherine Josephine stared at Mrs. Mackenzie blankly, who then patted her back and affirmed.

"Your children adore you, and your husband cherishes you. You have a wonderful family."

"I'm simply blessed. I can't wait to see them."

"You will, Katherine Josephine, you will."

Mrs. Mackenzie continued fixing up her hair and face. Both were silent. Katherine Josephine faced the mirror, looking at her reflection and, suddenly, pointed— "That's me!" She was so excited.

Then she asked, "Where are my babies?" She became tense.

"Downstairs with Edward Ferdinand," Mrs. Mackenzie answered.

She was finished. She extended her hand. "It's time now."

Katherine Josephine sat and stared in the mirror. She laughed and looked at Mrs. Mackenzie, "Thank you for taking such good care of my babies."

She nodded and smiled. They descended the stairs.

Everyone looked at Katherine Josephine, beautiful and lovely as always. They were ready to say their goodbyes. They were smiling, trying to stifle their tears, as they did not want Katherine Josephine to see them cry. She did not want them to be sad. She wanted them to remember her with love, and love always. It was hard, but they did it for her. It was her wish for them. To live their lives. They knew it, and that she would always be in their hearts: physically gone, but alive with them in spirit. She would forever be loved and remembered, never forgotten. Not ever.

Katherine Josephine faced her children. First, toward Susannah Joy, whose hair was up in a bun, with curled tendrils hanging down the sides of her face.

"Susie!" she exclaimed. She hugged her daughter. They held each other. "My darling daughter!"

"Mama!" she cried out and kissed her cheek. The two of them remained in that position for a few seconds. Then, she took both her daughter's hands, stepped back, and remarked, "You like to write, don't you? Perhaps you can earn a living doing that. You are so talented. Any company would be lucky to have you in their firm."

No one corrected her, but Susannah smiled at her mother. "Of course, Mama, I know."

Katherine Josephine released her, turned to Don, and put her hands on his shoulders, sizing him up with her eyes. "And you, young man, who might you be? Susie's boyfriend?"

Don smiled. "I'm her husband."

"Why, you're so handsome," she remarked with gaiety. He had impeccable, wavy, dark brown hair, and his clear blue eyes were gleaming.

Katherine Josephine put her hand over her mouth and laughed with embarrassment, "Oh, I'm so sorry. Please forgive me," she threw her head back, her hand still covering her mouth.

"Don't worry, it's all right. I forget things, too," he stated nonchalantly.

She then asked him, "What do you do?" She paused, stood, and stared, her eyes looking around. She was embarrassed.

Don, still grinning, answered, "I'm a lawyer."

"Oh, that's simply marvelous." She laughed again.

Everyone observed her. Katherine Josephine had not lost her sense of humor and spark.

Katherine Josephine turned to Andrew and Paige.

"And you," she stated matter-of-factly, "you're my son." She paused again, in a trance.

He offered, "I'm Andrew, Mom." He had grown up to be such a doll, with dark hair, perfectly combed and parted on the side. He gazed at her lovingly. He went over to hug and kiss her. She was surprised, and said, "You were very bashful as a child." She took his hands and said, "But look at you now. You are so handsome. I bet you have lots of girls fawning over you."

Again, no one corrected her. *Let her be. She is happy. That is good,* everybody reasoned.

Katherine Josephine went on, "You like animals, don't you? You had a pet hamster once. Right?"

Andrew nodded in agreement. At least she remembered that.

She saw Paige flanking her son. "And you, my girl. You are so pretty. You have any boyfriends?" She laughed, throwing her head back.

Paige did not get insulted. She was not that type of person. She knew Katherine Josephine had a memory loss disease that took away her ability to remember anything. She always loved her mother-in-law, and she loved her back.

"Mother Clock," she grinned, "I'm Paige, your son's wife, your daughter-in-law. We always got along so well."

Katherine Josephine stood in her spot and said nothing. No one did. But, again, that laugh. "Oh, of course, honey."

Susannah walked up to Andrew and asked, "Should we get the children? Mama ought to see them. They're dying to say hello to her."

Andrew agreed and called across the room, "Chloe!"

A ponytailed teenage girl appeared. "Yes, sir?"

"Bring in the children, please. Let them say hello to their grandmother."

"Of course," she obliged, and went back into the kitchen.

Andrew faced his mother. "Would you like to see your grandchildren, Mom? They have been waiting all day to see you. They're so excited."

Katherine Josephine's face turned into a blank stare as she said in a confused voice, "Grandchildren?"

Susannah and Andrew looked at each other helplessly. Katherine Josephine did not recall having any.

Susannah piped up, "You have three—two girls and one boy."

Katherine Josephine clapped her hands with joy and smiled gleefully, "Oh yes, oh yes." She was ecstatic. "Where are they?" She looked, puzzledly, back and forth, around the living room.

Suddenly, three high-pitched voices called, with their arms out joyfully, "Grandma, Grandma!" They ran toward her. The girls first. Then, Sean, who was very shy, but had obliged. Katherine Josephine looked at them. She was in a dream and just stood. "Grandma! Grandma!" they exclaimed again. The three of them threw their arms around her neck and kissed her cheek. Katherine Josephine was stunned but did not push them away. She did not want to offend or insult them, though she racked her brain trying, wanting, desperately, to remember.

She giggled nervously and patted their backs. "My darlings!" she remarked matter-of-factly.

Then she turned to Ariana and asked her, "And what is your name, little girl?"

"Ariana, silly Grandma!"

"I'm Donna," Andrew's daughter offered.

Then Sean stated, "I am your grandson, Sean, Grandma. Don't you remember?"

Still giggling gleefully, Katherine Josephine convincingly replied, "Of course, my darlings. I was just teasing you."

Again, everyone watched and said not a word. They thought among themselves, *she's still funny and witty. Just like in the good old days.*

Andrew then began, as he walked up to the children, "It's time for you to all go now. It's late." He looked at his watch. Then, to the babysitter, he called, "Chloe!"

She appeared, wiping her hands with a dish towel, and looked up. "Yes, Mr. Clock?"

"Get their hats and coats and take them to the car. There are books for them to occupy themselves, okay?"

Chloe nodded and led the children out of the room. They had been told their grandmother was suffering from severe memory loss. Susannah and Andrew did not feel they should tell them that their grandmother was going to die by assisted suicide, as they were too young to understand. Perhaps when they were older, they would be informed but, for now, all they had to know was that she had died. That was not a lie, they had thought, logically.

Everyone waited for the children to leave.

Edward Ferdinand walked up to his wife and stroked her hair. She turned to him. Both did not say a word for a few seconds.

He took her face in his hands and gazed lovingly at her. She stared blankly. Following suit, she reciprocated his gesture. They stayed that way for a moment.

"My queen," he called her.

Hesitantly and slowly, with a slight smile and twinkle in her eyes, responded quietly to him, "My king."

They both kissed each other lavishly, as they always had.

"I love you, Edward Ferdinand."

"And I love you, Katherine Josephine."

A few seconds later, he remembered, ". . . Katie Jo."

They both giggled because they thought it was funny.

Then they turned to their children. Susannah and Andrew stood together, watching their parents during their last loving moment. Their parents smiled at them, "Our prince and our princess, forever."

Katherine Josephine eyed the children who were about to weep. "Don't cry, my darlings. Shed no tears for me." She stopped, trying to go on. Edward Ferdinand supported her. "Remember me with love or don't remember me at all," she ended softly and quietly.

Katherine Josephine released herself from her husband and stated firmly and lovingly, with a smile, "I love you all."

Edward Ferdinand and the children concluded, "Forever and ever and a day." They returned the smile, blew her kisses, and waved. She reciprocated, for the last time. It was over.

The two attendants came downstairs and announced, "It's time now."

Susannah and Andrew watched. Edward Ferdinand stood like a stone as the attendants took Katherine Josephine's hands and slowly led her upstairs.

"Goodbye, my darling."

He spoke softly in a loving voice trying not to break down, for he knew she wanted him to remember her with love always and forever.

She turned and smiled at her family with a sparkle of love in her eyes.

The attendants turned and faced them. "We'll let you know when it's over," they stated, deadpan, then led her up the stairs to her bedroom and closed the door behind them.

Everyone watched and then sat down. No one said a word. They knew not what to say. They all knew the end was inevitable. She was going to die, which had been what she had wanted for herself and her loved ones. She did not want them to give up enjoying their own lives, which they were entitled to, to care for a permanently mentally crippled family member, who would never recognize them. She would get worse, and end up as a vegetable. She could not do that to them, and they understood completely, though they never considered her a burden or a responsibility. She always took care of her family, asking for nothing in return. She was supportive and thoughtful toward everyone, and they loved her for her selfless nature toward others. And now, in death, she was the same person—caring and considerate. Whatever she did, she did for love. Love for her family. And her friends. She would die, but she would always be in everyone's hearts, forever. Her love would never perish. She would go on living after her physical, bodily death.

Suddenly, they heard a voice.

"Time of death: 8:23:45 P.M."

It was over.

The technicians packed up the machine and equipment. Dr. Cornell and the attendants left the bedroom and headed down the stairs. Everyone on the couch looked up, their faces grave.

"You could call to have her body moved to the morgue and plan the funeral," Dr. Cornell flatly stated. Then, he added, "I advise you do it soon."

Edward Ferdinand nodded and agreed, and then faced his family. "That is it, folks. Let us get started."

They went.

THE FUNERAL-A WEEK LATER

The sky was a clear blue. The sun was shining brightly. The trees were fresh and green, and swayed in the breeze. The grass was watered and mowed finely. A perfect day for a funeral. Katherine Josephine would have loved this gorgeous day.

Before they watched the casket go lower and lower into the ground, they took a moment to remember how she looked before the lid was shut. The family gazed at her lifeless body and thought, happily, *she is so peaceful.* She was as beautiful in death as she had been in life.

Though everyone remembered Katherine Josephine's words to shed no tears at her demise, they had to struggle to hold back any signs of sadness.

But their desire was to honor her wishes, so they forced themselves to be in control.

Edward Ferdinand said to his family and friends, "She's at peace. She did it out of her thoughtful demeanor—her unconditional love for all of us. We will never forget her, and she will be in our hearts always. She loved and was loved."

They all agreed with him.

Edward Ferdinand thanked the minister for all his support and help during this dismal, trying time. Everyone shook hands, hugged and kissed one another, and patted each other's backs, sharing their deepest condolences.

Edward Ferdinand had his whole family come over to his house for coffee and snacks. He did not want to be alone, and neither did they. So off they went.

A YEAR LATER

Life went on for the Clock family, just as Katherine Josephine would have wanted it to.

Edward Ferdinand retired at age sixty. He sold his business to a young man, who had his own family. Susannah and Andrew agreed that they should sell their family home, which was filled with joyous, loving memories. Since Katherine Josephine died, it would not be practical for their father to live in such a big house by himself. It would be hard for him to maintain its upkeep and would also be silly, at his age, for him to pay such exorbitant property taxes.

All his wife's clothes and shoes went to Goodwill. Her jewelry went to Susannah. Her animal antiques went to Andrew. Her photo albums were for Edward Ferdinand. All the furniture was sold.

Susannah and Andrew found their father a retirement community project where other senior citizens lived. He would have his own quarters. His rent and living expenses and food were reasonable. He had a cleaning service come once a week. He did his laundry in the building basement.

He had no desire to ever remarry or even date a woman. He was not interested. To him, Katherine Josephine was his only one and true love, as well as his best friend. And although she was gone, he still felt that being with any woman, whether in a serious or platonic way, would be cheating on her. He had DVD recordings of him, Katherine Josephine, and their children, which he would watch when he was feeling lonesome. He kept a photograph of Katherine Josephine next to his nightstand. Every night, he would talk to the photograph and blow her a kiss. His family understood and respected his wishes completely. He met with other widowers, and they would talk of their beloved deceased wives, as well as their children and grandchildren. They played cards and bingo, and listened to country music on the radio. They enjoyed watching sports on television. Also, they went to the pool and clubhouse.

Edward Ferdinand continued to be close with his children and grandchildren. They visited him, and he took them for rides in his station wagon. Susannah Joy became the chief editor of the magazine firm where she had first started as a filing and typing clerk. She wrote and had a book published about Katherine Josephine. Its title was *Mama: Love You Forever*. It was not a bestseller, though it did sell well. She did not care, as she had just wanted the world to know what a wonderful, loving mother Katherine Josephine had been. Her husband, Don, started his own law firm, which was doing well, and he had two associates working for him. Their daughter, Ariana, was almost six, and could not wait to start the first grade. She was looking forward to it immensely. Andrew began his own veterinarian clinic, with two part-time assistants, and was happy. He had always loved animals. His wife, Paige, became co-owner of the bookstore where she had first begun as a part-time assistant. Their children—Sean, nearly ten, and Donna, going on seven—were very happy, delightful, high-spirited children.

Most important, there were two new joyful additions to the family. Susannah and Paige had their babies within two days of each other. They named them after their grandmother. Susannah had her daughter first. She had fluffy red hair, and Susannah named her Katherine Josephine, but would refer to her as Katie Jo, as her grandmother had preferred to be called during her final days on earth. Then Paige had a son, also with red hair, though it was thin and straight. He was named Kevin Joseph. Both babies had their grandmother's sharp, dark, gleaming eyes.

Though their babies were a lot of work and they hardly slept due to colic, diaper-changing, cuddlings, and feedings, they were a joy—and adorable.

Now, Edward Ferdinand had five grandchildren to love and spoil.

Susannah and Paige called and confided in each other sharing stories of their babies. They were best friends, in addition to being sisters-in-law.

Andrew and Donald also had good rapport with each other as brothers-in-law. They conversed about their totally different businesses. They bowled and played golf together.

One warm summer day, the Clock family decided to visit Katherine Josephine's gravesite. Ariana, Donna, and Sean were eager to put blue carnations, their grandmother's favorite color and flower, on her gravestone. They skipped up to the stone and laid their flowers down. They delightedly spoke in unison: "We love you, Grandma, forever and a day."

Edward Ferdinand and his children watched the three of them with pride. They were growing up so fast, and were so happy and well-behaved.

Susannah and Paige, holding their babies, strolled up to the gravesite. Susannah looked lovingly at her new daughter, as Paige did at her new son. Both smiled at their babies while trying to direct their attention to their grandmother's grave. Then, liltingly, they pointed out, "See that honey, sweetheart? That is where your grandmother lives now. In heaven, with the angels. She loves you very much. Can you say 'hi, grandma?'" Naturally, they knew that they were not old enough to comprehend them, but the two sisters-in-law were jubilant and satisfied as they giggled into their babies' tiny faces gazing at them with love. Then, while standing in front of Katherine Josephine's grave, they smiled and said, "I love you." They turned and walked away.

Then, Andrew and Don walked up to the gravesite and said, "Love you always and forever." They headed back.

Katherine Josephine's stone read, *Katherine Josephine Parke Clock, a.k.a. Katie Jo. Loving Wife, Devoted Mother, Beloved Grandmother. Rest in peace. We love you. You loved and were loved by all. Always in our hearts forever.* Blue butterflies, her favorite insect, because of its bright colors and slender figure, surrounded the stone.

As they headed toward the car, Edward Ferdinand turned and faced his family. "Who wants to go to Seabreeze Amusement Park?" he called out.

"Me, me!!" his three grandchildren shouted out loud. Edward Ferdinand motioned to them. Everyone piled into the car. They were ecstatic and full of joy. It was going to be a great day for all.

As they left the cemetery, they remembered the last words Katherine Josephine had spoken, firmly but gently, with much love and a smile, her eyes bright: "Remember me with love or don't remember me at all." They all did so. Forever in their hearts.

Edward Ferdinand switched on the radio to a country-western station that played Katherine Josephine's favorite song, "Louisiana Saturday Night." Everyone, though singing off-key, with high-pitched voices, smiled and swayed to the music, leading the band, laughing with delight.